RETURN to the WILDS

This free book and the accompanying writing workshop, led by author Cindy C, were made possible through the efforts of Altrusa International of Yaquina Bay and donations from the Siletz Tribal Charitable Contribution Fund and other community partners.

Email : Altrusainternationalyaquinabay@gmail.com

RETURN to the WILDS

a novel

CINDY C.

NEW YORK

LONDON • NASHVILLE • MELBOURNE • VANCOUVER

Return to the Wilds

© 2019 Cindy C.

Published in New York, New York, by Morgan James Publishing. Morgan James is a trademark of Morgan James, LLC.
www.MorganJamesPublishing.com

The Morgan James Speakers Group can bring authors to your live event. For more information or to book an event visit The Morgan James Speakers Group at www.TheMorganJamesSpeakersGroup.com.

Publisher's Note: This novel is a work of fiction. Names, characters, places, and incidents are either products of the author's imagination or used fictitiously. All characters are fictional, and any similarity to people living or dead is purely coincidental.

ISBN 978-1-64279-170-9 paperback
ISBN 978-1-64279-171-6 eBook
Library of Congress Control Number: 2018950129

Cover Design by:	**Interior Design by:**
Rachel Lopez	Megan Whitney Dillon
r2c design	Creative Ninja Designs
r2cdesigns.com	megan@creativeninjadesigns.com

In an effort to support local communities, raise awareness and funds, Morgan James Publishing donates a percentage of all book sales for the life of each book to Habitat for Humanity Peninsula and Greater Williamsburg.

Get involved today! Visit
www.MorganJamesBuilds.com

To H.G. McKinnis, fellow author and lifelong friend: relentless coach, mentor, muse, native guide and "sag" crew on the quest to fulfill my childhood dream of writing fiction. This book would not exist without you.

prologue

I n a thousand cities, automated war robots clicked and whirred, coming to life. In secret silos, panels slid open and gleaming missiles emerged, programmed to seek and destroy every kind of living thing except one – humans.

If Counselor Dred and his warbots aren't stopped, it will be the end of the Wilds forever. And the agreement that Keren and her friends just made with the world governing council to save the Wilds will be for naught.

Keren can't imagine a world without the Wilds and the Wildings who live there. Dred and his robot army must be stopped. But how can one girl, a few other children, and a handful of Wildings save the Wilds?

chapter one
FIELD TRIP

W AAAAAAAAuuuuuhhhh!

WAAAAAAAuuuuuuhhhhhhhhhh!

Creatures gnawed and buzzed in Keren's brain. She woke in cold fright—which melted into angry annoyance. Blowers! She sprang from her bed and peered outside.

Sure enough, the workers started early, chasing every leaf and grass blade from driveway to gutter, removing disorderly Spring from the tidy manicured urban enclave. They chased around persistent scraps of leaves still issued by the modified Gen trees.

When do we get the "Leaf Off" trees and lose those blowers? Keren wondered.

The touted new "Leaf Off" trees photosynthesized through bark instead of leaves. She'd seen the promo viz in OA Biology. Keren thought the spiny, thorny plants were kind of cute—like huge green spiders.

She tried to wrap on a robe while plugging her ears against the caterwauling. "Mother!" she yelled, thundering down the stairs for dramatic effect. She burst into the breakfast nook where Mother sat, drinking her morning coffee. "Why do they have to do this stuff so early?"

"If you would wear your HEAD, you could tune out the noise," Mom noted, adjusting her own Hearing Enhancement Audio Device. "You really should wear it to protect your hearing, dear."

"Why don't they turn down the city noise?" Keren retorted. "We've known for a century that it damages hearing. Babel is addicted to binge growth, and it's killing us. I am so tired of the roar and crash. Why is it grow, grow, grow?"

"Economic growth is the engine that drives prosperity," Mother recited. A bit of cynicism in her tone? Hard to tell. The woman was pro-business. Keren's parents owned a small artist supply shop and hung out with a free expression crowd. They didn't totally buy the growth thing, did they? Keren pressed her point.

"Okay, we have inalienable rights to economic prosperity. What about the right to a 'walkable, livable community'? What happened to 'Every Babelite is entitled to an environment free of excessive noise'?" Keren asked.

Mother smiled. "Is that from the World Code of Urban Rights?" she asked. "For a young person who despises urbanity, you seem to know a lot about it!" she teased.

"We pretty much memorized the world code for OA Civics," Keren explained. "And there's another danger from HEADs. The Dominion can issue subliminal messages. They are brainwashing you!"

"What a sinister thought," Mother said. "On the positive side, HEADs do provide a community connection, a virtual village. You can walk down the street and meet a neighbor, in your HEAD!"

"People used to walk in the neighborhoods and stop to gab with each other on the street." Keren recalled a class on small town life they had studied in history last year.

Mother looked wistful, her eyes gazing off in the distance. "It seemed more personal and spontaneous. You never knew who you might run into. Now we always know. And our store, Anderson Arts, is one of the last small stores where you might meet a neighbor, and...someday we will be gobbled up by ArtCorps Inc."

"The mega-development will wipe out your business, and wipe out Dad's art," Keren said. "The Dominion wants to stomp out all pocket parks and urban Wildlings. Then what will Dad paint?"

"His Nature's Notes are best sellers," Mother said. "A few of us like our urbanity with a touch of life." She pondered. "You think the Dominion is out to eradicate nature? Is that what Dr. Dierk is teaching you?"

"Dr. Dierk doesn't accuse them, he just relates the facts." Keren defended her favorite teacher. "The fact is, Urban Wildling Services is eliminating millions of squirrels, birds and rodents every year.

"And *that* is the main and final reason I won't wear my HEAD," Keren concluded, using her newly-acquired debate skills from OA Public Speaking class. "I want to hear the Wildlings in the City. I want my bird songs and squirrel chirps live, not simulated!"

She offered her final salvo. "The Dominion only gave us all HEADS so we would forget that they are replacing Nature with one big construction site."

"I make big noise," blurted Keren's little brother, bursting into the kitchen. He spun around and backed towards his sister shouting "Ding, ding, ding, ding."

"Stop that, Tug!" Keren screamed. She covered her ears as the toddler marched backwards swaying his arms and clanging at the top of his lungs. Tug loved big, noisy machines, especially oversized construction tractors with their clanging safety signals. He had learned some new noises from his Construction-Site Simulation package, gift of doting grandparents for a third birthday. Now he could play excavator or crane operator on a mega building site. And better yet, annoy his big sister. Tug's loud adoration exasperated the quiet-loving Keren.

"Tug, do you want some cereal for breakfast?" Mother asked the little nuisance.

"I want, I want Fuel Flakes!" he cried, receiving a bowl from his mother and clambering up his little footstool to reach the cereal delivery spout.

"How about you, Keren?" Mother asked.

"Can I have something without GMOs?"

"So you don't like our bioengineering marvels guaranteed to eliminate world hunger?" Mother teased. "They are pretty bland. We can't buy everything from Farm and Gardens." Keren knew her parents made sacrifices to buy a small stock of expensive health farm products. "I'll make whole-grain hot-cereal," Mother said. "While you get dressed."

Keren jogged back up the stairs to replace robe and tunic with pants and shirt. She checked her wrist tab to make sure she had programmed in all the readings and assignments for the day's lessons, then put a few snacks in her daypack. She flipped a message to her best friend, Caleb. *Meet you at Auto Corner 0730; watch out for blower boys!*

Caleb's return message popped up on the tab's virtual projection screen. *You ready for Wild pretest?*

Ready! she flipped back. The dreaded and adored pretest readied Over Achiever (OA) Biology students for the spring field trip. Each one-week trip explored a different Wild outside the environs of Babel II 4.1. The test helped students prepare for any dangerous situation they might encounter.

The Wilds experience transcended anything in urbanity; students had to be ready. Dr. Dierk did not need some kid frizzing out and getting the whole Wilds Field Trip Program shut down. Keren loved the meticulous details of field trip prep: checklists of supplies, safety protocols, the warning system, and the pretest, which plunged students into a simulated Wild with all its exotic sights, sounds, smells and apparent dangers.

She recalled Dr. Dierk's explanation of the Wilds Protection System. As the Babels expanded through the earth, new laws protected the last remnants of nature from urbanization. The officials labeled all parks, natural areas, and reserves "Wilds," exempted from urbanization.

The pretest exceeded the actual field trip for sheer challenge. Aided by the simulator, each student got lost in the midst of a different Wild—a barren mountain pass in subalpine tundra, a dense forest, a hot desert of blazing sun and cactus—with various perils to teach the right safety response. Keren knew how to escape from an angry mountain goat and avoid a buzzing rattler. What would Dr. Dierk spring on them today? Tropical Wild, she'd bet. Very scary.

She joined her family at the table, wolfing down her cereal topped with peanut butter and soy milk. Dad, eating grains, kept nodding appreciatively at Tug's scrawled drawing of an excavator. "We build mega mansion," Tug explained, grubby paws gesturing to stick figures hovering above a blobby machine. "I drive Excavator and Da makes blueprint on his tab. You think it, we make it," he said, quoting a favorite ad from the Noblitts & Nard BuildEarth Empire.

"Speaking of thinking, how did the pretest studies go last night, Keren?" Dad asked.

Keren pushed back her chair. "My eye is still recovering from the bee sting, I removed 100 leeches, and a spider monkey bit me," she answered. "I've programmed avoidance strategies for vipers, adders and cobras; and I've been testing mosquito repellants vs. meshes...but Dr. Dierk will surprise us."

"I wanna cober, Daddy!" exclaimed Tug. "Can I have a big 'nake? Buddy's big brother has a black 'nake in a glass box. He feeds him little ratties. I help him once!"

"Stay safe and watch out for snakes!" Dad's grin indicated that human varieties such as Yessers and Tattlers might be more dangerous than simulated animals in the Tropical Forest Wild.

Keren placed her bowl in the sink, made a quick round to plant kisses on her parents' cheeks and her brother's soft hair, and ran out the door into the roaring city. To take her mind off the noise, she thought about the Wilds Visit. To that first time, when everything changed.

chapter two
FIRST VISIT

Two years ago. The first Wilds visit. It almost didn't happen.

Dr. Dierk insisted they travel on a large vehicle he nicknamed "the Magic Bus" or just "the Bus." In his youth, he explained, students took a school bus for field trips.

"I applied for self-propelled transport," Dr. Dierk told the class. "Babel II 4.1 has a fleet for official Dominion business."

Self-propelled? Off the Auto? The class was shocked.

"Can't we just use travel pods on the Auto and meet up at the Wild entrance?" someone asked.

"That would be less hassle," Dr. Dierk agreed. "But this is a community experience, and we should travel to the Wild together."

Clearance from Urban Transport Authority took weeks. Dr. Dierk projected each new e-form for class entertainment: Security Risk Assessment, Traffic Pattern Non-Conformance Plan, Safety Plan, Parental Permission Contract, and Non-System Travel Budget. Each student even wrote a Personal Justification for Non-System Transport, assisted by Dr. Dierk.

Finally, URB-TA approved a 50-person vehicle for the Purity Wilds Field Trip.

On a cool Saturday morning, the students found a gleaming "bus" waiting in front of the Middle Education Resource Center. "Put 'em here, kids," the driver said, indicating a stow space for their packs. They clambered aboard: kids, Dr. Dierk, and two parent chaperones. Rows of plush seats along a central aisle awaited their glutes. They filed up the aisle and plopped into soft cushions, looking out large windows in amazement. No individual climate nor destination control, no music favs; they shared space undistracted by media. Soon that space filled with laughter and conversation as the conveyance roared to life and lifted into the air above the MERC.

The Bus flew slowly across the predawn city, over steel towers and factory reservoirs that reflected morning light. Their destination appeared below them, an island of green rising from the crust of pavement and steel. Then the Bus slowed to a quiet grumble, descended gradually, and stopped before a massive gate. They had arrived at the entrance to Purity Mountain Wild.

Two armed Rangers walked up to the Bus as Dr. Dierk bounded down the steps holding out his tab, preprogrammed with a Wild Code he had spent months extracting from the Authorities.

"Code?" demanded one Ranger, holding up the Entrance Activation Device. Dr. Dierk smiled and touched his tab against the screen. With a hum, the great gates slid open and the Bus floated through.

Beyond the station doors, the foothills of Purity Mountain Wild rolled up to a high ridge capped by pine-covered peaks. Before them, a sign marked Purity Mountain Wild Ridgeline Trail; behind it a footpath wound up a canyon towards the foothills. The Bus parked, and the group tumbled out. The great gates hummed closed.

Dr. Dierk passed out water and snacks, as the Rangers gave a brief safety briefing. Then the group followed Dierk up the footpath, trying to match his long strides uphill. Signs of life—stubby vegetation, dots of bright flowers, a lizard darting under a rock—greeted them as they crisscrossed the canyon, winding upwards, skipping on stones to cross Purity Canyon Creek, a trickling stream of water. Scrub brush and white hardwood trees with lime green leaves gave way to scraggily junipers. The trail left the canyon and zigzagged up the slope.

Later, Keren's mind would replay these scenes: that first sight of Babel below, spreading in all directions from the wall surrounding Purity Mountain Wild; superior views above of ponderosa pine, waving grasses, and limestone rock outcrops. Hawks swooped in lazy circles, playing on thermals rising from the ridge. The beauty, the life, the warm sun on her skin, breeze tickling her face. The breathy shhhhhuhh of pine song welcomed their ascent to the mountain ridge.

One by one, members of the hiking party made their way up to Savannah Saddle, the first rest stop. "Break," Dr. Dierk called. They situated themselves, each choosing a log or grassy patch beneath the towering pines. Keren felt peaceful and calm, more at home than at any other time she could recall.

Dr. Dierk, uncharacteristically quiet, lounged against a pine log, eyes closed, breathing in the unfiltered air. The students refrained from chatter and the two chaperones seemed stunned; no one wanted to break the powerful silence.

Keren heard a gentle humming in her head or somewhere in the silence. She felt awe and joy, sensing more than the simple scene of shade, sun, trees and grass. No one reached for a HEAD; they listened for the song within the silence. A whisper? A rush of waters? Something here, not scary or strange, but something they somehow had all known all their lives enfolded them in the moment.

That's why we have the Moment of Silence at Church, Keren thought. That awkward time of shuffling papers, sideways glances, and slight discomfort when it seems like everyone is waiting for Someone to arrive, until the pastor's voice breaks in with the Prayer. Is this what the Moment of Silence is for? Are we listening for something?

Sitting in silence at Savannah Saddle, she felt the life in her body, her pulse elevated, a trickle of sweat running down her neck. The hint of butterscotch from the pines, filtered sun, singing trees. Something indescribable filled her spirit.

In their prework packet, the Ranger Service supplied a pamphlet on the natural history of the area: "Purity Mountain Wild: The Story Behind the Scenery." There is a story, she thought. There is something here. Not like a ghost story. Not scary or weird. But something missing from her life. Until now.

After that, she could always go there. Taking a quick turn into that story behind the scenery of her life. A place of refuge, a place of beauty and wonder. Where colors lived vividly—dazzling green grass and deep blue streams, red and yellow floral accents. Leafy trees swaying in the mild breeze, where the sun shone unfiltered and her skin felt energized. Nothing to distract or reprogram her senses. No jarring sounds drowned out by HEADS, no clanging construction, no whirring maze of Personal Destination Paths. Instead of orderly steel towers, a random array of mountain peaks. Instead of manicured Astroturf, clumps of grasses and sedges. A tumble of plants, rocks, waters—and it all fit, all harmonized; all was right.

And that sound. Where had she heard it before? As a little child, lying on her bed at night, listening to the waters humming in her head. But here in the Wild the soundless sound soared all around her. Not just in her head. Someone speaking? No words. But she felt welcome. Welcomed home.

chapter three
CONSPIRACY

C aleb leaned against the kiosk at Auto Corner. Tall for his age, he had already attracted interest from the Sports Department. But Caleb so far only went out for cross-country running (on sim-fields due to limited "country"). He liked to move across the ground quickly. Caleb and Keren's friendship grew from their preference for walking.

"Auto" referred to the Automated Elevation System that hurried individuals along through the vast canyons of high-rise buildings soaring into bleak grey skies. Each preprogrammed pod had its own artificial atmosphere tuned to the controls specified in the user's Personal Destination Key (PDK).

Students took the Education Resource Center (ERC) Autos to school as a safety measure; the Auto went only to the destination programmed by PDK into the kiosk. Only students and teachers had an ERC code on their PDK, with temp codes issued to parents for official visits.

Keren and Caleb always met at the Auto, and then walked to school, working their way around racing ribbons and high-rises downtown, and passing through their beloved Puddicombe Pocket Park. HEAD-less and free-footed, they heard bird calls from the Gen trees and sometimes spotted a feral cat or rat slinking around a corner. Despite the ceaseless eradication efforts of Urban Wildlife, nature persisted in the city.

"Do you think we'll work as teams or go it alone this year?" Caleb asked.

"Every year is different," Keren replied. "It seems like if you plan on something, Dr. Dierk makes sure you experience something else. I thought we might get lost again so I downloaded maps with waypoints on my tab—but it probably will be a king cobra encounter or a downpour!"

"Dr. Dierk is a wonder," Caleb enthused. "We lucked out getting a ranger dropout."

"Not a dropout, Cal, he just got out when their mission shifted. Don't you remember? He started as a ranger biologist, studying the unique flora and fauna in a whole bunch of Wilds. That's why he knows so much," Keren reminded him.

"No offense," Caleb offered, seeing Keren's flush and realizing he had crossed a line, teasing about her science hero. "I meant that we lucked out getting a former ranger—someone who knows stuff, didn't just read about it. When the Ranger Service dropped exploration and conservation, Dr. Dierk dropped the Service."

"Right. Dr. Dierk thinks people need the Wilds or we lose something about being people."

They arrived at the portal to the Middle Education Resource Center (MERC) 1102, pressed personal IDs against the entrance pad, and the gates slid open. They trooped past the Safety Approved Playground (SAP) to join the silent throngs entering school. Most kids listened to music favs on their HEADs. Keren and Caleb often got strange looks as they gabbed to each other instead.

Dr. Dierk always gave the pretest first thing in the morning. Surviving its challenges left students energized and ready for the rest of the day.

As they entered the biology lab, Keren observed the simulator switched off and silent in the corner. Dr. Dierk stood at the podium, waiting for everyone to fill in the seats. His bony face looked sad and anxious.

"Where are the packs for the pretest, Dr. Dierk?" someone asked from the back.

"There is no pretest," Dr. Dierk said. "I am sorry, guys, but we will not be taking the field trip this year. There will be no visit to the Tropical Wild."

A stunned silence followed.

"Effective today, the Dominion has banned all field trips and other Wild visits until further notice," Dr. Dierk explained. "And planning a Wild experience has been designated a Potential Crime against Urbanity."

Dr. Dierk raised a hand to stop the hubbub evoked by his announcement.

His rangy form looked awkward in the neat shirt-tie-collar and pants attire of a Teacher/Analyst (TA). He was the only person Keren knew who still wore eyeglasses or "spectacles" as he called them. Behind those glasses, his grey-green eyes clouded with concern.

"Students, the Wilds are in great danger. We need to help them," he said. "This moratorium on Wild visits is part of a larger movement to dismantle the Wilds entirely."

A coalition of Progressives, developers, and Dominationists had proposed a worldwide Wilds Development Protocol, Dr. Dierk said.

"Babel expansion needs Wild acreage," he said. "Developers propose mega-mansions on the high mountains and luxury resorts in specific ecotypes: alpine, desert, oceanic, arctic. Mega-millionaires will spend mega-bucks for great views and pristine enclaves."

Keren interrupted. "Isn't that kind of elitist, Dr. Dierk?" she asked. "Wilds only for the favored few? Wild experiences bought for a price?"

Dr. Dierk grimaced. "Supporters say Wilds development will enhance the economy and finance factory farms for reduced world hunger."

A student raised his hand. "What about the role of Wilds in maintaining the complex carbon and water cycles?"

The class nodded. They spent hours studying for the planetary cycles test.

"Only a handful of scientists and a few smart students like you know this," Dr. Dierk said. "Progressives believe exposure to unfiltered sun, air, and natural plants disrupts the human emotional balance."

"Disrupts how, Dr. Dierk?" challenged Caleb. "Humans evolved with the earth and its natural systems. Our ancestors lived off the land, and survived by learning the plants and adapting to the seasons. Our brains are wired for this exposure—we need the Wilds."

Dr. Dierk smiled. "We should send some of you to the Tri-annual World Administrative Convention," he said. "TRI-WAC vote on the Wild Development Protocol is scheduled for this coming Monday. I imagine that vote is hard-wired for affirmative."

His smile faded. "Based on recent history, I doubt facts will win this argument—even from you, our best and brightest.

"We've discussed the debates over human evolution in class. Progressives think urbanized humanity is evolving to a self-controlled state of detached equilibrium—something like what the ancients called 'nirvana.' Dominationists insist there is no such thing as evolution. Most people accept one camp or another without really thinking."

Keren felt sick to her stomach. Weeks of planning and anticipating an adventure faded into disappointment and angst. "Why does this stop our field trip?" she asked.

"The Dominion's Anti-Wild Visitation Directive keeps people out of the Wilds until the TRI-WAC ends. They claim that Wild visits create controversy and endanger public safety."

"The Dominion just wants people to forget about the Wilds so they can destroy them," said Keren.

Dr. Dierk sighed. "Who knows what the Dominion wants? The public has no access to its officials, let alone their motives. We only know what the Dominion does—at least, some of it."

"Can't we launch a protest?" asked Lizzie. "Remember how we stopped the Tussle Watershed Enhancement Project?"

"Save the Tussle!" shouted a couple of boys, pounding on their work platforms. Others stirred excitedly. "YEAH! Student power!" cried Todd and Tammy.

"The Engineering Authority planned to cut down the woods along Tussle Creek for an expanded flood control channel," Lizzie reminded them. "We went to the Precinct Council and took turns speaking about how the woods protected the watershed and the Council voted it down."

Dr. Dierk smiled at the show of support, but then said soberly, "That won't work this time. No way to get authorization this quick for cross-global transport and TRI-WAC admission. And I'm now under observation."

A collective gasp. Dr. Dierk—a marked man?

"It's Dominion Human Security," Dierk added. "DHS has added names of frequent Wild visitors and known Wild proponents to the Agitators List."

Keren had visions of dark-suited DHS agents slinking around the corners of the MERC, tailing Dr. Dierk on his pocket park strolls and reading his tab talk.

Her teacher's voice interrupted her fantasy. "I think we have a chance to counter this movement and save the Wilds. But it will take the courageous efforts of everyone here."

"Doing what, Dr. Dierk?" asked Lizzie.

"We can project Wild experience worldwide—using the simulator," Dr. Dierk said. "I already use projected simulation for the Wilds pretest. Every time I visit a new Wild, I pack sensors to record sensual updates for the simulator. Your pretest is an experiential visit to a Wild that impacts all your senses—sight, smell, taste, hearing, feeling.

"I have come to believe the sensors also pick up subliminal messages from the Wilds, only heard by the human spirit," Dr. Dierk added. "I can't prove it, but you all understand. I think you have 'heard' them."

"You mean the 'Sounds of Silence,'" suggested Marty, who collected ancient music auds and had an archaic music reference for every occasion.

"Something like that," Dr. Dierk said. "I can't explain this mystery, but when you enter a simulated jungle you not only see a tiger, large as life, hear its roar and smell its musky scent—your spirit also feels awe and sense of Something your ancestors knew, a sense of universal order."

"What do we do?" Bopha, no-nonsense and practical, wanted specifics.

Dr. Dierk explained. OA Biology class could team up with brainies from OA Physics and Engineering to project simulated wild experiences along the World-Wide Grid.

"At a given time, we'll project Wild sights, sounds and subliminals to every available HEAD. People will suddenly experience the Wilds with all senses, physical and spiritual," Dr. Dierk said. "This jolt of awareness could shock people out of their blind trust in economic progress and urbanization. No guarantees, but we can try."

Irving Fidget, the king of geeks, rapidly drummed his fingers, intrigued. "What if we send the strongest simulation dose to the people pushing Wild development? We track them down by meta-search and hack into their personal profiles." Master hackers, Irving and his buddy, Cynthia Cyber, started as toddlers tabbing the vast reaches of the Grid—public and private. They spent much of their free time roaming the alternative cyber universe.

"Intriguing," said Dr. Dierk. "Taming-the-Wilds Coalition members and delegates backing the Wild Development Protocol would be logical targets."

"We could find other anti-Wilders among the Dominationists and Progressives, and maybe in corporate and wealth creation factions," suggested Paul Wonk, who loved the complexities of power brokering.

"We'll get their HEAD code," Irving said. "No problem for you social networkers to get us names and Grid addresses."

"That might be illegal," Dr. Dierk worried.

"Not technically," Cynthia reassured. "Free ranging on the Grid is cold gold; in fact it's a right of 'individual expression' protected by law."

Paul Wonk buzzed his tab. "Excuse me. Individual rights date back to the World Cooperative Accord. The Accord built these rights into the fabric of our international society."

"Do you guys remember how we got the Accord? Nations' obsession with national security and national interests had provoked wars in every sector. Every nation had nukes to blast—they had a choice between world peace and World War III. No one wanted another world war. So they got rid of the nations."

"And your point is?" interjected Lizzie, yawning loudly.

Undeterred, Paul continued. "The Cooperative Accord established the Babel System: numbered by continent, state or province, and municipality. Ours is second continent, fourth state, primary city so it's Babel II 4.1. One world, one Babel, committed to peaceable prosperity and growth."

"You sound like a Dominion promo blurb," Lizzie said.

"Actually, people fear world dominion," Paul countered. "That's why Individual Expression, Civil Society, Gender Equity and Rule of Law are so jealously protected—and the Dominion is charged to protect those rights."

"Well, this is pushing my proposal into new dimensions," Dr. Dierk admitted. "TAs should set examples of public cooperation—not engage in espionage. But—"

"In an emergency—use extreme tactics!" Caleb quoted Dr. Dierk's Wild manual, projecting confidence class-wide. Irving and Cynthia high-palmed and grinned, others smiled or conferred excitedly. Keren's angst turned to fragile hope.

"We have a very short time to pull this off," Dr. Dierk said. "We have projection capacity for one surge from MERC 1102. If we line out codes and program the simulator by Friday, we can send the surge after delegates arrive at the convention."

This year's TRI-WAC would convene in Babel I 1.1 on the former Asian continent. Delegates would come from all over the world, traveling on Saturday.

"The Holy Convocation, traditional start for the TRI-WAC, is on Sunday," Dr. Dierk continued. "That's when they vet the Wilds Development Protocol, and that's when we send our simulator surge."

"Why aim for Sunday start-up, Dr. Dierk?" asked Bopha.

"The Holy Convocation sets the pace for the whole TRI-WAC," Dr. Dierk said. "Paul, you tell us why it's so important."

"When the Worldwide Cooperative Accord established the TRI-WAC, they debated the start day," Paul Wonk said. "Some countries lobbied for Monday as the first work day, but Babel II reps wanted Sunday. That's when business conventions usually start. They also had some cultural superstitions about the importance of Sunday. Since they invested the most Capital, they won. Sunday starts the important work of world administration."

"And we can call it 'Surge Sunday,'" Dr. Dierk said. "We want the biggest bang for our buck," he added, evoking a few chuckles. His quaint sayings added to the aged teacher's charm.

"What do you think?" he added. "Are you with me?"

The class roared with agreement; most students jumped to their feet. "SURGE! SURGE! SURGE!" they shouted. "Save the Wilds! Save the Wilds!"

Dr. Dierk put his hands up and the hubbub ceased.

"This is serious stuff," he said. "A high-risk operation. Participation is not mandatory—it's a volunteer extra credit project. An opportunity to up your grade—but no penalties for those who elect not to."

Everyone looked around in amazement. Who would *not* fight for the Wilds?

Sissy Shirk and Timmie Tremor looked agitated and embarrassed. Keren remembered they each had a parent serving in the Yessers. Black marks for a family member could impact or even end careers.

"There are backstage jobs as well," Dr. Dierk offered. "I need volunteers to develop a background report on the Wilds of the world—establishment, natural history, visits, etc. This material will find its way into the briefing book for TRI-WAC delegates."

The timid twosome raised their hands in relief. They too could help the Wilds and not imperil their parents.

"So we'll use class time for the project this week—instead of our plans and prep for the Wilds visit, okay?" Dr. Dierk looked around at fifteen eager faces.

"Okay, let's get to work."

"YEAH!" The class shouted their agreement. Wilds work began.

chapter four
VANISHED!

 eren had trouble distracting her parents. Dad wanted to know all the details of the Tropical Wild pretest simulation. Of course, the simulation never happened.

"We took a wild motorboat ride through the mangroves," she invented. "We cruised by a fishing village; wide-eyed children just staring at us or running up and screaming 'Hello!' People live right in the Wild and the guys fish all day. We saw some of their funny boats; they waved and smiled as we zoomed by."

"Zoomed?" Dad raised his eyebrows.

"Our boat had an engine, but the indigenous people used oars. They go out to the middle of these huge tidal lakes to fish," Keren explained.

"And this year's emergency?" Dad asked.

"Well no snakebite, or leeches like I had feared—I got lost," Keren said.

"We stopped the boat for a little hike through the tropical forest. I started to readjust my wrist tab, and a monkey snatched it! While I ran after the monkey, everybody else headed up the trail...I had to find my way alone without SAT coordinates and only a paper map..."

She told the simulation as she imagined it, glad that she had done so much reading on tropical forests.

"Usually Dr. Dierk has sent us the trip manifest and pack list by now." Mother sounded worried. "This is just not like him."

He has bigger things on his mind, Keren thought. The class probably needs a plan for parental interference.

"Aw, Mother. This is our most exotic field trip ever," she said. "The Tropical Forest Wild is two continents away. We have a three-hour flight."

"You know there are zillions of details—Inter-Babel travel restrictions, Wildling protection treaties, personal safety requirements... Dr. D wants to have it lined out just right so everyone knows exactly what to do," Keren said. "We already did the preparation Biggies: Inter-Babel PASS, tropical disease immunizations, DHS Security Check."

"Poor Dr. Dierk is probably overwhelmed," Mother said. "Maybe I should offer some help—I'll message him..." Before Keren could think of a distraction, Mother had tapped her wrist tab to the Dr. D preset.

"Hmmm. No answer and his VM is on overload," Mother said a minute later. "Ask your teacher to call me, Keren. Tell him I want to help. You know I can organize anything."

Keren slipped out the door to avoid further inquiries or offers. She wanted to finish her task for the new OA project—programming sensory stimulation from bird calls: the strident *Whip-Puh-chrr!* of the whip-poor-will, the melodic *churteree* of a thrush in deep forest, the screech of an osprey.

Her mind full of bird song, she started at a sharp whistle from the Auto corner. "Caleb! You scared me!"

"You're just jumpy from all that programming," Caleb teased.

"How's the Projection work coming?" she asked.

"We've got the codes for central HEAD transmission. The Dominion developed this for an emergency alert system, but they never used it."

"Why did Dr. Dierk make you a Projector, Cal? You're not geeky," said Keren.

"My psychic ability helps the geeks sleuth out the HEAD Yesser code names," Caleb said. "Yessers tend to be certain personality types and make predictable code names. I've found some pretty stupid ones: SPY (System Protection Yes!). HIP (Hearing Improvement Projection). CIA (Code Instructed Agents). FBI (First Best Invaders)."

"System Protection Yes! How durky can you get?" Keren giggled. "I would rather have my head full of birds."

"Me too, but it's all for the cause, and Yesser minds amuse me," Caleb said. Then he looked embarrassed. Keren knew her friend shared her disdain for Yessers but also felt compassion. He had no desire to belittle anyone's soul, not even that of a Yesser.

They took an Auto pod to speed their way to the MERC. Hopping down the slider, they tapped their MERC 1102 portal codes, raced through the sliding doors, and headed for OA Biology.

Dr. Dierk had asked everyone to come to class a few minutes early each day for a brief preproject meeting to check team progress, and keep everyone on track.

Keren's heart sank when they entered the classroom. Instead of Dr. Dierk's lean frame, a flabby man stuffed into an Administrator suit stood at the podium, beaming.

Ugh. Mr. Snark, the Deputy Administrator for MERC 1102. He often imposed bureaucratic barriers to the Wild Field Trips. Not a welcome sight to the project team.

"Good morning Science Over-Achievers," said Mr. Snark. "You are here early. I understand you are working on a special project with Dr. Dierk. I am sorry to say that Dr. Dierk is indisposed and will not be at the MERC today. We have arranged for a Substitute to resume your General OA Biology lessons. But since we have this time before class, could you update me on this special project you all have been working on?"

Oh. Gawd. Keren's thoughts spun.

To her surprise, Timmie spoke up. "Mr. Snark. You know that all field trips to the Wilds have been indefinitely postponed. Dr. Dierk believes Wilds are very important. He launched this special project to update the simulator on all our Wild experiences so it can be used for future virtual visits available to all Babelites."

Would Snark buy it? Timmie had offered a plausible explanation but skated close to the project's true purpose. Caleb gave Keren a reassuring nudge.

"A science educator must 'keep all future options open for the benefit of civilization' according to the Educational Advancement Regulations, or the EAR," Timmie added. "In the future, our civil society may agree to a need for virtual visits to Wilds. The project will ensure we have this capacity."

"Thank you for the enlightenment," said Mr. Snark, his smile not reaching his eyes.

"So can we get back to the project, sir?" Caleb asked.

"Sorry, Mr. Benson. The project can be resumed at a later time, perhaps with Dr. Dierk's return. As Mr. Tremor mentioned, simulated Wild visits could be very useful.

"Today the OA Biology class will return to the conventional urban biology curriculum. Wilds now are a controversial topic, and I would not want to put your parents' careers or your records at risk."

"We're probably already on the Agitators List," whispered Lizzie, not quite loud enough for Snark to hear.

"What did you say, Lizzie?" Mr. Snark asked.

"I said I wouldn't want to be on the Agitators List," the perky blonde replied.

"We do not 'list' young people," Mr. Snark reassured with a phony smile.

"I would like to introduce your sub—Ms. Mincer, will you please come forward and meet your class?" They waited politely as a smartly-dressed woman clicked her way to the front.

"What a trend-head," Keren whispered to Caleb.

"I can hear her small mind darting around," Caleb whispered back. "She's clueless and harmless—but we can't progress on the project with her here. We need a new plan."

Keren felt her mind spinning with agitation as Mr. Snark outlined Ms. Mincer's teaching credentials. Where is Dr. Dierk? How can we save the Wilds now?

A sense of reassurance invaded her manic mind. Looking around the class, she saw other troubled faces beginning to relax. Caleb, she thought. The class psychic, priest and peacemaker. Words from an ancient Twila

Paris song sounded in her mind: "*This is no time for fear / This is a time for faith and determination / Don't lose the vision here / Carried away by the motion / Hold on to all that you hide in your heart.*"

Good thing they started with a Premeeting, Keren thought. What if Snark had found them actually working on the project?

chapter five
COMMISSIONED

C aleb.

Who's calling me? Caleb sat with a small cluster of friends. They picked dejectedly at their hydro-veg salads, complaining about the "airhead sub" and discussing daring plans to save their project. They talked in code, realizing the Yessers had tuned up the sensor system and possibly planted a Tattler in their midst.

The center filled with chattering students. But no one looked his way; no one hailed him from across the room. So who called?

Caleb.

He glanced at his wrist tab: nothing.

A voice in my head, he thought. Maybe *–Dr. Dierk!*

Caleb, tune in.

He visualized the rangy teacher, his energy, and the intense grey-green eyes behind the specs. Suddenly, they talked face to face just as they had so many afternoons in the empty Bio classroom, discussing ideas.

Where are you, Dr. D?

Doesn't matter now. Listen. We must save the project. You and Keren must lead.

What can we do?

Go to the Desert Wild and meet the Keeper. He, uh She, uh SHUH-HEE (S/HE) will show you what to do.

We have to go there? Can't we find the Keeper from here?

The Keeper is everywhere, but cannot be heard in Babel. The droning, the noise, the Progressive message is too strong. It drowns out Truth. Just as it drowns out memories of the Wilds. Only in the Wild can you see and hear the Keeper as S/HE is.

Why couldn't the Keeper come and solve this if S/HE had the answers and power?

He felt Dr. Dierk's gentle chuckle. *We have chosen to isolate ourselves from the Wilds and the Keeper honors our choices. But S/HE will help those who choose Truth.*

Caleb remembered Desert Wild from a class visit. It lay along Babel's western boundary. He recalled funky cacti, colorful birds, even a bobcat bounding across their path. But nothing supernatural.

I thought the, uh, the Keeper is somewhere out there, up there. Not out in the desert!

The Keeper speaks in the desert when people need to hear. When new truths and new ways are needed. Seekers have always gone to the desert.

But Dr. Dierk. You took us there on the "Bus." How do we get there?

Keren thought Caleb had lost his mind.

"Travel at night across the city?" she asked. "That has to be the craziest thing ever. Cross-urban travel is forbidden for unaccompanied minors. The Security Yessers are everywhere. We'll be caught on the Auto."

"We won't use the Auto," Caleb explained as they walked home on a circuitous route through pocket parks and hydro-gardens.

"We'll walk. That's why S/HE chose us. We are good walkers," Caleb said. "We can get across the Inner City to the Desert Gate by dawn. Dr. Dierk gave me the SAT coords for Desert Wild. We just have to map a route."

"Wait," Keren protested. "We can get to the Wild without a Personal Destination Key?"

"Oh yeah. The PDKs are based on the SAT coords. Before the Auto organized travel, people used satellite coordinates to plot their journeys," Caleb added. "Now a PDK locks into the correct SAT coord. They still use the coords for Urban Adventure Races."

"Come to think of it," Keren said, "I used SAT coords to create our nature route to the MERC. So I can make a map. Can you get supplies for the trip? We'll need snake med, water, a little food, sunblock..."

"We don't need provisions. Dr. Dierk told me our needs will be provided for."

Keren's practical side cringed. "Caleb, don't be such a mystic! We're not spirits. We'll get burned and bitten, and we won't survive long in that hot place without water."

"We'll find help along the way and springs in the desert," Caleb said.

They walked through Puddicombe Park. Unlike the shadowed city canyons, the park shone with bright spring sunshine. Keren stared at her friend in the rare sunlight.

Caleb's face glowed like a holy figure in one of the glasswork windows at church, (but without a plate behind his head). His whole being seemed to pulse with energy.

Her voice filled with surprise. "What happened to you?"

"Something touched me while I talked to Dr. Dierk," Caleb admitted. "Let me share it with you. If we move in this energy, we won't fail."

As they stood in the warm sun, Caleb caught Keren's hand in his. He focused on his encounter with Dr. Dierk—what he heard, felt and saw.

And then she, too, heard it, felt it and saw it.

chapter Six
URBAN JOURNEY

2 300 hours. Good thing her parents rose early and crashed early, she thought. Dad will be fried when he gets up and finds me AWOL, but we'll be at DW by then. The SAT showed 24.1 km across the city to the West Gate. Maybe five hours, but a little more time and distance to circle around Yesser Security, the Central Citadel, and the Dominion Palace Grounds.

For once, she did not bound down the stairs, but crept quietly.

An upstairs door creaked.

"Where you goin' Sissa?" Tug peered out of his door, small face beaming with adoration. "I go too?" He toddled down the stairs and threw his arms around her legs.

Tug.

The bane of her existence. Noisy, exuberant, and slow. His loud, shrill voice, "Look at *DAT*!" His short steps slowing them. Can*not* go. But how to stifle the little brat? He would pitch a fit or start whining, and her mission would be thwarted.

"Tug-shhhhhhh" she whispered, putting a finger to her lips. "Secret mission."

The little boy looked up. He solemnly put his finger to his lips. "Secret. Shhhh."

"We are secret agents," she told him. "You and me. I have to take a message to the authorities. And you, *you* have to guard the house."

"Guard house?" Tug's voice rose in excitement, then hushed as his sister once again tapped her lips. He pondered. Then whispered, "I get my MAR!" His proud possession, the toy military assault rifle, another gift from Grandpa.

Keren envisioned the small boy patrolling the house, MAR over his shoulder, perhaps shouting "Hup-To, Hup-To!" What assignment would get him back to bed—and back to sleep?

"Yes! Agent Tug, prepare your weapon. Put the silencer on. Secure the house. Check every window, door and entry. But you must be quiet as a tiger. If anyone hears you, the mission is destroyed."

Tug listened, enraptured, trying to stay quiet although his small body quivered with excitement. He made a stern face. Important, grown-up work.

"After your silent patrol, return to bed and await further orders. Be patient. This Mission may take a long time. Keep your MAR ready, but hide it."

She shook a finger. "If you are questioned, you know NOTHING. You do not know where I am. You do not know I left the house. You slept all night. Understand?"

Tug understood. "If they catch me on patrol, I say I sleepwalk."

Tug did sleepwalk and could carry on a lucid conversation when accosted. *"Where are you going, Tug?" "I go school" or "I go football practice."* "They will not catch you Tug, because you are a good spy. You are soooo quiet. You will patrol the house on tiger paws." Keren demonstrated, slowly walking on her heels and arching her toes/claws as she did for playing Zoo. "Tiger paws to prepare for your mission. Tiger paws on stealth patrol."

"Stealth patrol," he whispered. "Tiger paws. Yes Ma'am." He crept back to his room, as tigerish as a toddler could be.

Whew. Keren imagined her accomplice crashing loudly to the floor while attempting to balance on "tiger paws." She hoped he would fall asleep in the midst of his mission, curling up to dream of man-warrior glory. And, in the meantime, Tug would focus his energy on something he had never tried before—being very quiet.

Out in the street, Keren slipped into the shadows avoiding a group of Party Animals moving loudly along the sidewalk. "They must be high to be walking," she thought to herself. The Dominion had legalized minor stimulants; most adults accepted partying as a legitimate recreational outlet for bored young urbanites. Keren, however, did not want attention from a group of rowdies. She remained in monitor mode, something she learned observing Wildlings. She waited until the pack passed by.

They met at the Museum of Urban Growth (MUG). Keren hated the place, but Tug loved it: a tall shiny structure filled with replicas of soaring towers, builders and blowers. It housed a model of the intricate Auto web and a replica of the Earth, mapping real-time progress of urban growth and reduction in open land.

"Ew the MUG," Keren whispered to Caleb, as she joined him.

Caleb turned. He had been starting at the Space Tower—symbol of urban progress and the insignia worn by every Yesser.

"Soaring upward, onward, outward—progress always," he quoted the Yesser motto, just to annoy her.

"Cancer cells would be a better symbol for urban expansion," Keren responded. "But they aren't as greedy." She flicked her wrist and displayed the first part of their route—direct across the city except for jogs through Central City Park, pocket parks, arboretums, and community gardens. These provided cover for the journey and, best yet, Yessers avoided these places. They started walking. Keren filled Caleb in on her Tug encounter.

Caleb chuckled. "I can just see him marching around the house."

"On tiger paws," Keren said. "I couldn't let him come. My parents would phase. And he is so loud and slow."

Around them, the city roared. Construction and excavation projects worked through the night, lit by solar-power EEL (energy efficient light) systems charged during the day.

"I hate this noise," Keren said.

"Night construction is for citizen safety," Caleb reminded her. "The Build-Safe Regulations."

"Ah yes, the BS regs. Fewer people whizzing by Auto to collide with a construction crane," Keren said. "But the bright lights are killing birds."

They'd seen the alarming viz during an urban wildlife sequence. Birds falling like hail during fall and spring after the first mega-sky towers went up, lighting the night sky.

"It's sick," Caleb agreed. "The poor birds think they are navigating by moon and stars, but the artificial lights confuse them and they crash into buildings."

"Remember that awful dead bird collection trip?" Keren asked.

"Who could forget?" Caleb groaned. "I bagged 66 robins and 37 warblers. I could never be a bloodthirsty biologist like Dr. Dierk."

"Nobody wanted those birds dead, Caleb. The city killed them and we collected the evidence. That helped the birders push the Lights Out Initiative. Now they dim the night lights on mega-towers after midnight and have those sky cloaks strung up over the construction sites."

"That's good for the birds but what about us?" Caleb asked. "We can't see the stars. And look, it's 2350 and out here it's bright as a super sunny day."

They walked through the glare surrounding the Big Dig site. Huge excavators chomped away at the first cut of a system planned to undergird the entire urban complex.

"Big Dig," Keren said. "One hundred square kilometers underground."

"The Progressives hope we will all live underground someday," Caleb said. "This is their pilot project. Someday we'll all live safely in little burrows, free from weather or natural disasters. Like little moles."

"These are noisy moles." Keren winced at the KA-CHUNK! KA-CHUNK! of a giant excavator. "Tug should have come along after all. He'd be in Heaven."

KA-CHUNK! KA-CHUNK! KA-CHUNK! WHONK! THUNK! THUNK! WHOMP! Zeeeeeeeeeeeeeeeeeeeeeeeeeeeeee. Zeeeeeeeeeeeeeeeeeeeeee. Tup tup tup tup tup tup tup. Tup tup tup tup tup tup tup. Tuppa-tuppa-tuppa-tuppa-tuppa-tuppa-tup!

Keren plugged her ears and sped up the pace. "Those robo-hammers are the worst. With all our technology, you would think we could make something quieter."

"The inventions of humankind tend to be noisy, ugly and smelly," Caleb agreed. "At least when we are trying to exploit some resource.

"You know the Big Dig is being financed by the new minerals they are mining as part of the project," he said. "The builders claim they may make a profit. Ka-Ching!"

"What is Ka-Ching?" Keren asked.

"I have no idea," Caleb admitted. "Some ancient expression for the sound of money."

KA-THUNK! KA-THUNK! WHOMP!

The duo winced as the excavator bounced back, its gaping mouth filled with soil, rocks and tree roots, and launched its payload towards the fill pile.

They scurried past the site.

"Hey you kids! You shouldn't be so close to this site! You are going to get hurt!" A Security Yesser bustled up.

"With all due respect, sir, we are following the ped path," Keren replied. The path ran right along the site, separated only by a three-meter safety shield—translucent so passersby could enjoy the entertainment.

The officer blocked their path. Keren looked into a grim face with a blunt nose and small eyes behind night blades. He towered over them, big but flabby—probably a retired DHS Special Forces Agent retrofitting as a Security Yesser.

His eyes narrowed, almost vanishing into his wrinkled face. "What are you kids doing out so late?"

They had no curfew. Even Juveniles had Individual Rights. But Yessers protected security on construction sites.

"We are working on our OA Biology Project, sir," Caleb answered. He flicked his wrist tab and showed the guard a night bird mortality count. "We are curious about the effectiveness of the Big Dig Sky Net in reducing bird mortality. See, here are some pre-Net figures from the past three migrations..."

The "Zoh" (zoology) geek talk had the desired effect. Jowl-face stifled a yawn. "Uh, yeah, good. Do your parents know you are out here at 0010?"

"We have permission for the OA Biology Project," Caleb said, offering a reassuring smile.

He must be projecting confidence and authority, Keren thought. Mind-messing. But Caleb is skating close. She held her tab under the officer's nose.

"Call our parents to check if you need to," she offered. "But they work early schedules." She knew Yessers hesitated to impose on individual privacy and rest; it was a social gaffe in the densely populated, overworked city.

"No need," the Yesser agreed. "But I am buzzing this in to Central as a Pale Amber Alert. Big Dig is a High Security Zone. Aberrations must be reported."

"Yes sir," Caleb said. "I didn't know two preteen junior scientists would be much threat to Big Dig Security, but you have to do your job. We will move through as fast as we can."

Giving the Yesser a nod, he sped up, taking long strides away from the site, forcing Keren to jog to keep up. The officer frowned and tapped his tab.

The welcome quiet of Central City Park, one of the largest parkland remnants in the city, offered a refuge from the construction barrage. Central City Park still had natural trees.

"Thank Gol for Greenies and Outsiders!" Keren exclaimed. "They have kept the Central free of Gen trees and GEPs so far—despite the Restoration schedule."

"The Urban Restoration Project exempted the Central," Caleb said. "But most Greenies and Nature Heads are old folks. They are going to die out. The URP is just waiting for natural extinction."

"What will they do about us?" said Keren. "Our generation isn't going extinct, unless they poison us with artificial air."

Except for a few soft safety globes along the ped path, they walked in darkness and silence.

A whip-poor-will started up and continued an insistent chant, *Whip-Puh-chrrr! Whip-Puh-chrrr! Whip-Puh-chrrr!* The two friends paused.

"We're too far west for whip-poor-wills," Caleb protested.

"We have a Mexican Whip-poor-will," Keren corrected. "I just played the call today." She added, "I like this sound better than excavators and barking Yessers."

"Close call with the Yesser back there," Caleb said. "Now we are on the monitor."

"Quick thinking as usual on your part," Keren commended. "But a little misleading, don't you think?"

"Misleading, yes," Caleb said. "But not a lie. I never lie."

Caleb had strong personal ethics against lying.

"It is true we're working on an OA Biology project," Caleb continued. "Our parents know and support that. We just have shifted focus. Instead of planning a trip to a Wild Place, we are headed there, right now."

"What about the bird story you told him?" Keren pursued, inspired by the night bird's continual chant.

"It's also true we are concerned about night bird mortality, and interested in the effectiveness of sky safety nets. We just talked about that before we got to the Dig. I just flicked the Grid search on night bird mortality figures and for some reason, he lost interest."

"Oh Cal!" Keren punched his ropey arm as they strolled under the great oak trees along the path. They matched steps to the whip-poor-will call and chanted "Whip-Puh-CHRR! Whip-Puh-CHRR!" under their breath, giggling.

"Whippy wants us to hurry up and save the Wilds!" Keren giggled. "There aren't many parks left for him."

The march carried them through kilometers of parkland and then onto darkened residential streets. Their journey rang with bird calls— *Chip chip chip chip chreeee(!)* from the cardinal's rich repertoire, *Sweet-Sweet(!)* offered by the few thrashers who had survived the city death lights, *twerp(!)* from a worm-grubbing robin on the pseudolawn of suburbia, scolding grackles and the harsh *niyaaak(!)* of blue jays in the trees. Never had Keren heard so many birds.

She wondered if the Keeper had sent birds to encourage their journey. "Sure glad we don't wear those stupid HEADS," she said. "We would miss the concert!"

Other encouragements appeared. Although Keren had insisted on water bottles and vitality bars in their go-packs, they didn't need them.

They discovered little pocket parks along their route ringed with natural trees and each sporting a small water fountain bubbling like a little waterfall. The water tasted pure and fresh—not the usual recycled stuff. The trees smelled fragrant and bore golden fruit the students had never seen before. They couldn't resist a taste—delicious, like the soft sweetness of peach with a bit of berry tart, moist and refreshing.

Every time Keren got thirsty or a bit tired, a pocket park would be right ahead of them on their route, just in time for a brief break.

She wondered who designed these urban oases. She doubted that the city architects had planned for walking —the ped paths occurred sporadically, apparently designed for home-to-Auto transport.

Now they walked on deserted streets. The few commuters whizzing above them in the opposite direction seemed oblivious to the walkers below. Hearing the whoooooosh of Auto passage, Keren sometimes glanced up and saw faces, half-asleep or focused on wrist tabs, flashing by.

Energized by mystery fruit, watered by the fountains and encouraged by bird song, she led their steady march across Babel.

In an underground vault near City Center, two Security Yessers watched a real-time city map and two glowing amber dots moving towards the western boundary of Babel II. "So this is the Pale Amber Alert from Sector V," the grey-haired supervisor observed.

"Yessir, Officer Bulldog buzzed it in at 0020 and we have tuned city sensors to monitor ped movement in western sector. Definitely moving towards the western border and the Desert Wild."

"Two kids walking towards the Desert Wild? Why?"

"From the vector buzzed in by Bulldog, they could be OA brainies from MERC-1102. Dierk's Nature Heads."

"Dierk!? That detractor? I heard about him at the morning briefing on Pre-TRI-WAC Security Concerns. Dierk's on detention for safety protection purposes. Why don't you run the bios? See if you can positively identify—"

"Already attempted sir," Sweasel replied. "Central System is down—again," he noted with a grimace. "I propose we activate a Western Sector security force to apprehend them before they leave the city. It is temporarily restricted to enter a Wild, sir."

"I know that, Sweasel. But it is not restricted to walk across the city. At least not yet—we are working on it. It's so subversive and anti-Progress to walk but it's still a protected Civil Right. We don't want a mocking column in the *Babel Babble* about hyperparanoid Yesser Security forces arresting kids. Especially right now with the stir over the Wilds Development Protocol at the TRI-WAC.

"With the system down, we can't identify them as Dierk's students. It's impossible that he sent them, since he is incommunicado. If we had a positive ID, we could pick the kids up as a favor to their distressed parents and deliver them home, but I'm not wasting resources going door-to-door in the MERC-1102 commuting area to find out which OA students are missing. We are skating close to violating Individual Citizen Rights.

"We're three hectoseconds into the next shift and I cannot authorize OT—we will need it for inevitable civic unrest over the TRI-WAC discussions. I'm ready to hit the Auto. I hate these night shifts." He yawned. He noted frustration on his subordinate's face and added a suggestion to divert Sweasel's endless energy.

"You want to donate some OT, you can stay on and confirm their trajectory. Then alert the Desert Wild Rangers. It's their job to keep the unwanted element out of the Wild."

He unfolded his bulk from his EASE (Ergonomically Adjustable Seat Extension), gave the younger man a nod, and lumbered out of the monitoring center towards the Auto port.

Sweasel's face flushed. One more promo opportunity screwed up. Geez, these retired-on-the-job supervisors! Now the Desert Wild Rangers would get the inside shine for containing the security risk. His finger hovered over the security alert tab on his board. So easy to be the hero, so close, but he couldn't risk another noncompliance pan. The Supervisor did little, but he wrote meticulous reports.

He worked over the screen coordinates a few more hectoseconds. Then he flicked his wrist for direct connect to the Desert Wild "PRO" (Park Ranger Office).

The western sector felt warmer and dryer; a faint odor of creosote wafted on the air from the vast desert lands beyond the Western Gate. Builders had pounded and pulverized the formerly rolling landscape of arroyos and sand dunes into a flat, barren wasteland crisscrossed by roads and long rectangular buildings.

The welcome smell of desert in the air dispersed into odors of chemicals and scorched rubber. The cacophony resumed as Keren and Caleb entered the Far West Industrial Sector (FWIS), skirting long warehouses ringing with loaders, lit factories humming with machines, and transport trains roaring back into the city. To Keren, the FWIS seemed an angry creature that roared, groaned and screamed as it assembled, processed, fabricated and transported all the raw materials of urban progress around the clock.

No ped paths here, so they made their way cautiously along the curbside gutters, wincing as a large loader nearly ran them off the remnant roadway as it scurried towards a large warehouse.

"They sure designed walking out of this sector," said Keren.

"They want us to walk on the indoor Treds with Sim," Caleb said. "Why bother with nature? You can have it on your own terms. Just program in any nature experience you want to enjoy—without all the nasty annoyances like weather, wind—"

"Or that terrible *crack* natural trees make when 'removed' to make way for progress," Keren agreed. "Well if they make it hard enough, people will stop walking outdoors."

"This little burb used to promote its pedestrian-friendly walkability," a voice joined their discussion. "But then the burb fathers decided that development generates income—walking does not. They gave up on their ideals—and then rezoned the burb for higher priority industrial development."

They turned in surprise to the voice. A thin, slightly bent old man observed them from his perch on an antique lawn chair. His chair occupied a scrap of desert pavement in front of an ultra-thin "towny" squeezed in between two large industrial buildings. The man wore a fancy dressing gown that Keren recognized from ancient fashion photos as a "smoking jacket." He looked to be at least 100, a real oldster, clear blue eyes regarding them with interest from deep pockets in his lined face. Like Dr. Dierk, he wore spectacles.

"You live here?" asked Caleb.

"Oh yes, I am a holdout. They couldn't get me to sell the family place when the FWIS went in. They filled in Desert Swamp Wash. They took all our lovely ironwood and desert acacia trees and transplanted the cactus gardens to the Bio Type Museum. They filed an appropriation order to get most residential property in West Desert Burb. But they didn't need our little 'towny' space, as we successfully proved in the Land Court. So here it is and here I am."

"I bet you have seen some real changes, Mr. uh..." Caleb said.

"Mr. Watcher," the old man replied. "That I have, that I have." His blue eyes bored in. "But what are you young folks doing out here in the FWIS way before dawn? This is no place for young people."

"I don't think it's a place for any people," Keren agreed. "Isn't it unpleasant for you? Living here? Watching them haul away your burb, your life—piece by piece?"

"You are an insightful young lady," Mr. Watcher said. "I have watched them haul it away and replace it with the noise and metal and clang of progress. For the last 30 years. But it's real," he added. "It's history. It beats transfer to the Elder Assistance Center to be fed, numbed and placated 'til I die and stop blocking progress. And it gives me something to write about."

"Write?" Caleb asked.

The old man tapped his wrist and the virtual keyboard appeared.

"Back in the day I edited and published the *West Desert Weekly*. The West Desert Burb no longer exists. But I still put out *WD Monthly* on the Grid for my amusement—and for my declining audience of faithful readers. Most of them are in elder centers now and of course they are dying off. But they want to know about the old neighborhood."

"We are doing an OA Biology project on urbanization problems," Caleb said. "We wanted to get through the FWIS before daylight, before it really gets busy and even more hazardous for foot travel."

Questions formed on the old man's furrowed forehead. Mr. Watcher appeared to collect himself. "Don't let me detain you young folks from your mission," he said politely. "Maybe you can give me a lead on it later, for my next edition."

"You must know a lot of history on this area, sir," Keren noted. "Could we contact you if we need some background for our project? What's your tag?"

"Glad to help," the old reporter said. He directed his wrist tab towards Keren's. A buzz and she had Mr. Watcher's tag and profile.

"Well, he *could* be an asset," she told Caleb as they hurried on. "He certainly is *not* a Progressive. And he doesn't buy what's going on here. Plus I'd rather leave with him feeling useful rather than suspicious."

"I don't think he'd buzz the Security Yessers but he might gab about the two young people who walked by his house before dawn today. We might even get a mention or photo in his next *WD Monthly*." Caleb sighed. "But I don't think we can prevent that."

"Did he get our photos?"

"Sure did. I think he wrist-flashed us when he first saw us—before we noticed him. But I don't think he'll give them to the Yessers. If he's an old-school journalist, he sees himself as the watchdog against Authority. And he never reveals a source."

"But if he did," Keren said, "they'd identify us as Dr. Dierk's students and pick us up."

"There's the Desert Gate." Caleb motioned to the steel wall. "We have a good shot of getting through. If we can get past the Rangers."

chapter seven
BAD RANGERS

Head Ranger Shirl narrowed her eyes and pursed her lips, round face scowling, annoyed at the news. Young Nature Heads on the boundary of Desert Wild—her unit. Any more bad news and her career would die.

Since her transfer to this godforsaken outpost, Shirl faced down one negative issue after another. Last month a rattler struck Deputy Mayor Strident during the yearly Yesser Desert Tour. Friends of the Wilds staged a huge protest when she cut maintenance on Saguaro Loop Trail—a ploy to counter budget cuts that blew up right in her Gen-restored face. Now this risky Wild Development Protocol. It could boost protection, fatten the development portfolio and establish "service fees." But it also meant outside scrutiny and internal strife. Shirl oversaw an uneasy blend of Biologists, Rangers and Engineers. If the TRI-WAC passed the WDP, one staff faction would win and others lose. Shirl disliked power imbalances. For now, the Wild Visit Moratorium must be enforced correctly and visibly.

She touched her wrist.

"Ranger Knot, we have an unauthorized visitor situation. Please assemble an interception team at the East Gate."

Shocked awake by tab buzz near his berth at 0545, Ranger Knot first thought "Wildfire!" One of his major security problems: fires from the flammable, invasive grasses moving from Babel into the Wild. *Wrong season* he realized as he tapped the tab. His supervisor's voice filled the room as the viz showed her war-painted countenance.

Knot disliked Head Ranger Shirl but acknowledged her political skills. Knot hated political games. Let someone else play them.

As Shirl gave orders for the unauthorized visitor situation, Knot smiled. He barely restrained his exuberance.

"We will manage and contain the threat," Knot assured his boss.

The lead VCR (Visitor Control Ranger) had started as a young Parkie charged to conserve and protect parks from unruly Visitors. The message behind every portal sign, kiosk and list of Rules: "NO!" Knot loved visitor situations.

Knot now worked for a reinvented Ranger Service that administered all public lands—reclassified "Wilds." Most of his colleagues hated the streamlined mission but Ranger Knot found it reasonable: Rangers protected the Wilds from people.

Knot thrived in Visitor Prevention. He oversaw Interpreters, Conserver Biologists, and Visitor Control Rangers (VCRs). Interpreters taught visitors to respect the Wild, Conservers studied Wild resources threatened by humans, VCRs enforced visitor rules.

Now, the ultimate unauthorized visitor situation offered itself. "We're on it, Head Ranger," he said.

Desert Gate slowly slid open. Keren and Caleb walked through.

The transition zone from Industrial to Desert featured a cactus garden and a Visitor Interpretive Center (VIC), an attractive adobe building displaying murals of desert creatures and plants. The Park Ranger Office (PRO) sprawled behind it.

In the predawn light, the desert rolled away from the park ranger complex in gold and grey hills dotted with rock piles, scruffy bushes and spidery green stalks of creosote. A few saguaro stood like sentries. A mourning dove called: *Ooh WAH hoo, hoo hoo.*

Uniformed Rangers marched out of the PRO, forming a line between the visitors and the Wild environs. The Rangers wore clay-brown uniforms. Their shirts sported badges with the Babel tower superimposed on a saguaro, their trousers were tucked into neat brown boots to allow easy movement through desert brush and thorns, and each belt holstered a stun gun. Keren recalled the Ranger maxim was "Never harm—only redirect." She hoped these Rangers agreed.

"The welcoming committee," she said and wondered *what now?*

Caleb heard. "I will make a way in the Desert," he recited. They stopped. And waited.

"Young Visitors. Desert Wild is closed until end of the Tri-WAC." Knot stepped in front of the cadre. He needed to be careful here. Visiting Wilds was still an Inalienable Civil Right; the visitation restriction had been promoted as only a short-term security measure. These students must be handled with civility.

"What are you doing out before dawn and how did you get here?" Knot asked. "You're violating a Dominion order and endangering your safety."

Caleb met his gaze. "The Desert called us," he said. "And we came."

Nature Heads, Knot thought. Probably Dierk's kids. That dropout. Indoctrinating the youth, making them as crazy as he is.

He motioned and two Rangers moved up alongside the young duo. "This place is restricted. We must redirect your Wild visit."

Keren and Caleb paused before the hard-eyed Ranger. Fight or flight? Keren wondered.

Stand firm she heard from beyond the cacti.

"Come along, young lady." A woman took her arm. Her partner grabbed Caleb. They tried to hustle the kids towards the office.

Nothing happened. Their charges stood rooted to the earth. Keren felt nothing, yet the larger woman turned red in the face.

Her colleague tugged on Caleb. "Unnnng," he grunted.

"Reinforcements!" Other Rangers moved in with stun guns drawn; one raised a large net used for Wildling capture.

A mourning dove called and was immediately joined by others into a great choir of mourners. Rangers stopped and listened.

Ooh WAH hoo. Hoo Hoo. OOH WAH HOO. HOO HOO. OOH WAH HOO. HOO HOO.

Strong winds swept down, stirring up sand into a hundred dancing dust devils. Keren stood, assailed by wind. Dust devils occur in the flats— not the foothills—except today! Gold sand flew in spinning whirlpools. Whirling air and dust knocked the rangers to their knees. They covered their eyes as their bodies flailed around, buffeted by invisible forces. But Keren and Caleb remained rooted to the ground.

Come! Someone called to them. A small furry creature moved towards them, creeping beneath the currents. It briefly stood up on its hind legs, motioned with a paw, then turned and moved off, its cinnamon fur bristling in the wind, bushy tail waving like a tattered sail. "Coatimundi!" Keren whispered, delighted to see the desert creature with its long striped tail. She realized that the dust devils whirled a few feet above the ground—a physical impossibility—and the coati moved with ease through a pocket of still air below them.

The temporary paralysis ended. Both Keren and Caleb could move; they dropped to a crouch and crawled along the ground beneath the whirling wind. They followed the waving tail past the Rangers into an arroyo behind the compound. Muffled shouts and roaring winds faded behind them.

They won't be hurt noted their guide as he sauntered away from the commotion. The winds subsided, and they jogged behind the bounding coati, his tail a merry flag. A dust devil could rage up to 20 minutes. Time enough to elude the Rangers.

Their furry guide squealed softly, and she heard *we will be far into the desert, away from any Rangers.*

"The Keeper chose to meet us out here because it's undeveloped?" Caleb asked.

It is a safe place to meet, Coati agreed. *But S/HE always speaks to people in the Desert.*

The quote formed in her head: *I will allure her into the wilderness and speak tenderly to her.*

"You are one smart coati!" Keren said.

The animal halted and stood up; its long face seemed to smile. *There is wisdom for any who listen.*

Coati moved to the foothills of a rocky mount. Now they climbed up the mountain.

"Won't the Rangers track us?" Caleb asked.

"They can't get very far," Keren reminded him. "No copters, electronics or SAT in the Wilds—even for Rangers. Until the Wilds protection laws, Rangers claimed they needed air and land trans to fight fires and search for missing persons."

Caleb chuckled. "Or for fugitives. Now the Rangers must hike to track us down. Thank the Keeper for Rule of Law."

The morning sky shaded pink and yellow. As they climbed, the desert landscape stretched out before them: gold hills and washes, green accents of bush, trees and cacti. To the west, rolling hills graded into sky. To the east, Babel graded upwards from flat industrial warehouses to residential hi-rises and the Central City towers.

Desert Gate, where concrete and steel met sand and plants, control met disorderly life, and artificial met natural. Keren's heart lifted; she stood on the Wild side.

As they stood at the rocky pinnacle, looking down, the mountain seemed different, fully on earth yet seeming to stretch beyond it.

They sensed presence and power. The Keeper.

chapter eight
KEEPER

WELCOME.

A being that seemed to be cougar, fawn, and desert tortoise—all exceptionally large—stood before them on the mount.

"Are You ALL the Keeper?" Keren asked.

YES. All the Animals spoke but only one voice sounded. WE ARE ONE. TODAY WE COME AS STRENGTH, GENTLENESS, AND WISDOM.

"You met Us earlier this day at the entrance," the Tortoise spoke, the grim line of its mouth opening into a smile.

"In the dust devil?" Caleb asked, eyes wide.

"An odd name for Our Spirit," the Tortoise agreed.

The Cougar became prominent as the Tortoise faded behind her. "Your kind has always wrestled to understand Us," She said. "Younger ones learn faster, so We chose you."

"Chose us for what?" Keren asked.

"We will send you to divert your kind from destroying the remnants of the Wilds. You need their beauty and life. Humankind cannot live without the Wilds."

"But Great Keeper, You can do anything, why don't You stop it?" Keren asked. "You could just remake it all. Or maybe a flood—"

"Been there, did that," the Fawn said and enlarged into feline form.

"The time to restore is not yet," the big Cat's eyes glowed with fierce light despite Her calm voice. "Your kind must learn the limits of human power. This is your assignment—your share in the human mission." She stopped and licked a huge paw.

"This is the season for changing hearts." The Fawn's dappled form emerged. "Your kind can change. Every shift of intent, every heart softening, and every choice for life—these energies merge with Ours to restore all things."

"In this world," added the Tortoise, "We do all things through your kind... with your willing cooperation or through your rebellion. This is why your kind feels responsible. You are. More than you can ever know." Its voice rumbled through the great green shell.

Keren felt a chill. "We're just kids! What can we do?"

She recalled stories about the Keeper's nasty habit of sending people on impossible missions. People with any sense tried to get out of the assignment.

A chuckle from the shell. "The words of the Prophetess will guide you. Wildlings will come to show the great Babels life and power," the Tortoise said.

"You will bring the Wilds to the people and the people to the Wilds. What your mentor began, you will complete."

"Dr. Dierk! Where is he?" Keren asked.

"He will lead the war of words, once you free him."

Keren's heart fell. "Dr. Dierk is in prison? Is he okay?"

The Tortoise's ancient eyes focused on her. "Dr. Dierk is detained. He has not been harmed. But you will fulfill his mission. You must go for Us."

"But first it's time for refreshment," said the Cougar. "You traveled far. Come enjoy the fellowship of the Keeper and feast with the Wildlings."

She turned and trotted away, and they followed Her down the mountainside, leaping over rocks and brush. Coati loped along behind them, descending the mountain in graceful bounds.

chapter nine
WILDLINGS

They entered a wash narrowing into a red-walled canyon. The rocky wash turned to sand; a small stream ran along its middle. They waded in cool waters surrounded by towering cliffs and trees. An opening revealed a grassy flat ringed with majestic cottonwood trees.

Caleb and Keren gasped.

It seemed that every desert critter from *Flora and Fauna of the Desert Wild* had gathered to welcome them. Many families—foxes and kits, bobcats and kittens, coyotes and pups, javelinas with piglets—assembled on the grass. Mule deer with spotted fawns stood behind them. Ground squirrels, kangaroo rats, wood rats, jackrabbits and ring-tailed cats rested on their haunches. Birds filled the trees: hummingbirds, quail, doves, cactus wrens, and woodpeckers. The great predators, hawks and owls, perched on the branches. Collared lizards and horned toads arranged themselves on the rocks at the edge of the meadow, basking in the morning sun. Several large rattlesnakes also coiled on the rocks, beautiful diamond patterns glowing, rattles quiet, as the visitors sloshed onto the grassy shore.

How could this be? Keren's biology brain floundered. Predator and prey gathered together and sitting quietly.

She heard a chorus of voices—chirping, rasping, snorting, grunting, purring and buzzing— "*Welcome, friends and keepers.*"

Did she hear this somewhere inside herself? In this place she could understand Wildling dialect.

Their Escort faced them, the animals behind Her. "We have summoned Wildlings from this place to greet you. Welcome to Our home where all life lives in Our harmony," She purred. "Welcome to the feast of the Keeper."

The circle parted to reveal the feast arrayed on flat rocks: wood bowls filled with spring water, cooked prickly pear pads and saguaro fruit (somehow spineless), roasted pinon nuts, steamed palo verde peas and sautéed cholla buds. Mesquite bean bread beside a stack of clay bowls. Enticing smells beckoned.

How did they make all this? Dr. Dierk once talked about *Using the Edible Plants of the Desert.* Her mind clouded with a vision of bobcats and jackrabbits pounding bean pods into flour, baking bean bread on a hot rock and boiling the peas over a fire—what kind of container did they use? How could they do woodworking and pottery with paws and hooves? Then a less scientific question: *Why feast now when we have such an urgent mission?*

The Cougar paced toward her. "All time is Our time, and in this place the present moment extends as long as needed. Rest and enjoy Our provision."

Somehow the Keeper's time also made summer and fall plants available for a springtime meal. Something else to ponder.

Caleb and Keren sat on the grass, munching bread, cacti fruit and vegetables. Their hosts also ate. Deer browsed from shrubs, mesquite beans and acorns set out for them. The more nimble coatis, raccoons and ringtails assisted predators and hooved javelina filling up their bowls. Keren gaped at bobcats and snakes feasting on beans and peas rather than their normal meal of rats, rabbits or other small critters. Maybe out of politeness to the guests? She had read of predators eating birdseed, fruit or even vegetable matter left in people's yards—back when people had "yards."

Caleb the pacifist always claimed the Keeper only made life, not death, when Keren argued the biological necessity of predation and decay to maintain ecological balance. He said balance had been lost, but would be restored and then all life treasured.

The morning air felt fresh and cool; scents of spring flowers, oily creosote and the piney honey fragrance of cottonwood buds perfumed the air. The humans sat on the cool grass, leaning against a white sycamore log. The babble of the stream mingled with animal chatter: a blend of squeaks and little barks. The mechanical din and sterile air of the city seemed like a hazy dream forgotten in the peaceful morning.

To dine with Wildlings, to watch Coati's clever paws clasping a bowl, see young fawns spring up like dancers, hear the short barks of a fox family conversation: a dream come true for her young biologist's heart. These animals looked and sounded like fauna she had studied as long as she could remember—but seemed larger, more vivid than the furtive creatures she had observed darting behind rocks or plants on Wild trips or in nature vizzies. They seemed relaxed and confident in the presence of their Keeper Who threw back her head and roared with laughter, showing giant incisors, amused by the comments of a coyote seated beside Her.

Keren could understand the animal conversations. She couldn't tell if the words formed in her head or in her ears; she heard squeaks, grunts and barks, but if she tuned in, she understood. Two young female coatimundis crouched near her, clutching prickly pear fruit, taking dainty bites. "How do you get your tail so glossy...?" asked the red-coated female. Her tawny-gold companion preened and puffed out her massive tail. "I use jojoba oil; you just groom it in and...whooooeee...!"

A couple of rattlers sunned themselves and boasted about encounters with humans. "He went for my rattles," said the large male, coiled up in mock alarm. "But I bluffed him, made a dash for it and..."

Scientific questions formed in Keren's mind. She leaned towards the snakes. Just then the Keeper approached Caleb and made a graceful bow, head dipping between her paws. "Shall we dance?" She purred. To Keren's amazement, Caleb leaped to his feet and took a large paw in hand.

The Great Cat and the boy whirled and spun; the Cat perched on her hind legs, large tail twitching as they promenaded, do-si-doed and did a variety of steps Caleb knew from folk dance class. Somehow the big Cat followed his "lead" with amazing gracefulness, twirling Her tawny body.

All the animals leaped to join the dance: an intricate set of leaps, bounds and twirls. Keren found herself swept into motion, feeling a joyous spinning sensation, twirling around and around until she felt dizzy. She followed the whirling, jumping company: deer, canines and felines leaping and bounding around the meadow; birds swooping in and out; lizards and rodents scurrying back and forth among the larger animals; and even snakes weaving quickly along in the grass.

Energized and joyous, they all followed the Great Cat: bounding over the grass; bouncing off rocks; flinging themselves over logs; skipping, jumping and dancing around the clearing; even splashing into the stream where dace, chub and other fish joined the dance, leaping through the air and back into the stream. Leopard frogs jumped into the water, swam a few breaststrokes, and hopped out to join the land dancers.

As they danced, Keren felt a greater Dance encompassing them. She sensed multitudes of beings dancing, leaping, whirling. Some looked human and others were larger and brighter. The dance grew to encompass fiery orbs, gaseous clouds, bright light and dazzling colors that moved in graceful arcs and fractal patterns. A symphony accompanied the Dance: chorus of bird songs, frog calls and other voices merging into roaring waters, wailing winds, chiming stars and clopping comets. A song beyond knowing, joined by all. The clearing merged into a great expanse that appeared like endless waves of glowing white clouds, greater and vaster than anything Keren had ever seen on air trans flights: endless expanse. *Space isn't dark and gloomy.* She wondered why the orbiting Space Scopes did not capture these lights, unimaginable patterns and the glorious expanse. *Your technology cannot visualize Greater Things,* she heard.

Refreshed yet gloriously exhausted, as after a hike in the Wild or field day at the MERC—Keren and Caleb flung themselves down on the grass. Their hosts had departed; only the Cougar remained.

"And now We can send you," She said. "In the strength of Our food, in the power of Our vision, in the memory of the Great Dance."

chapter ten
SENT

T hey stood again on the desert mountain, in early dawn once more, as if no time had passed. Morning colors moved across the cityscape—lighting up the towers in hues of orange and gold. The Keeper in Fawn form stood on a rock, looking solemnly over the scene below.

He turned towards His guests. They rose to their feet and gazed into large brown eyes. "Are you ready to go for Us?" He asked.

Keren would have preferred to stay in the Desert Wild.

The Fawn gave a bleating chuckle. "It would be good to stay here forever," He agreed. "Someday you will join the eternal Great Dance, beloved daughter," He said. "But not yet."

"Now you must speak for Us to your people, children," He said. "If they listen to you, humankind may exist on the planet a little longer."

"What do You want us to do, Keeper?" Caleb asked.

"Return to the city and your school; tonight you and your friends will free Dr. Dierk from the Citadel. My Wildlings will be readied for a great gathering. You will complete the Wilds Simulation your teacher planned, and broadcast it worldwide—on the morning of the Opening Ceremonies, from the TRI-WAC itself.

"Everyone who dons a HEAD will see and know the power and glories of the Wild Earth. Shock the hearts and change the minds of your kind, and save them from destructive forces they have unleashed."

Keren's mind spun. "Wait, wait! How do we get back? How can we free Dr. Dierk? How can we get to the TRI-WAC?"

"As you go, We will help with details." The Fawn winked. "We will provide transport and disruptions."

A thundering scream and a WHUMP WHUMP WHUMP above them interrupted His words. A huge lizard-like creature with flapping wings slowly descended to the mountain. The hilltop shook as air currents from the creature's descent buffeted them, and nearly knocked them off their feet.

"A dragon?" Caleb asked, eyes wide and mouth open.

Keren's feelings of terror cooled to scientific interest as she corrected, "It's a Quetzalcoatlus, the biggest flying reptile. But it's extinct!"

"Only in your time, child," the Fawn replied. "Everything We create continues to live in Our presence. Every life force remains available for Our purposes. Your mission requires reminders of the glory and power of Life in your world. Your kind has forgotten fear."

No wonder the ancients wrote of dragons and sea monsters, Keren thought. The Aztecs even worshipped something that looked like the large feathery beast that now folded its wings and stood on the rock between the children and the Keeper. It towered above them all, a bird monster with huge wings slack at its side, a small crested head atop a long neck, long sharp beak and cold green eyes observing the nervous humanoids.

Sitting back on powerful haunches and dipping its long graceful neck it bowed to the Keeper.

Crrrrrrrrkkkkkkkk! it cried, *Glory to You, Most High. What do You wish from Your servant of ancient times?*

"Take Our little keepers home and return to yours, but stay ready for their summons," the Fawn said. To Caleb and Keren, He added, "Do not fear, little ones. The task is tremendous. But you will receive help when you need it. In this world, We work through those who are willing. Are you?"

Keren recalled the glory and joy of the Great Dance. "We are," she said, and Caleb nodded. She addressed the Quetzalcoatlus. "Take us home."

The Quetzalcoatlus crouched lower and unfurled a great wing. Keren and Caleb inched up the incline and sat in a space between the two great wings. They heard a soft cry and saw Coati scampering up the wing behind them. He held two water sippers. *For your trip,* he said.

How did the animal get packaged water? Maybe from the Rangers' encampment?

She heard the Keeper's laughter in her head. *Ponder Our provision, beloved biologist. Until We meet again.*

The coatimundi bounded away, disappearing into the brush. The ancient reptile dipped its head to the Fawn, and with a great bound, leaped off the mountain. For a terrifying second they dropped like a shot, then the great wings caught the thermal currents off the mountain and they soared high.

They flew over Babel II, only a few lights marking the darkened city beneath them. Unlike the hover-trans or rockets, their "vehicle" moved quietly with only an occasional whump of wings. They scattered a flock of terrified birds, but their mount remained focused on her mission.

Time moved backwards; only a sliver of predawn light showed.

Keren's wrist tab indicated 0600—about the time they arrived at Desert Gate. Their entire Desert Wild visit had occurred in an attosecond. How? She remembered the Keeper's words about time. She didn't understand. Perhaps time condensed or moved in another direction in the Keeper's World? They would get home before anyone woke up. But what about the Yessers? Had the winged reptile triggered urban defenses? Would they be shot out of the sky?

Sweasel shook his head in disbelief. "Are you sure?" he asked.

The Head Ranger's face filled the monitor, flushed with anger and frustration. Behind her, a rumpled Ranger Knot rubbed his eyes.

"Ranger Knot's detachment met intruders at East Gate. But a disturbance immobilized the interception team," Ranger Shirl said.

"A dust devil," Knot explained. "Never seen one in this environment and certainly not one this big. Sensors did not detect it. It disabled the team and the intruders disappeared."

"Have you searched the Desert Wild?"

"As soon as we recovered—I dispatched personnel, mounted and on foot," Knot answered. "We found nothing."

"We cannot use aerial reconnaissance in the Wilds at present," Ranger Shirl interjected. "A full sweep detected no human presence Wild-wide... as if they never had come."

A grim face appeared on another monitor. "Air disturbance above Sector V," the officer reported.

"Give me a visual," Sweasel ordered. "Stand by, Rangers," he ordered. He gasped as the monitor filled with a terrifying vision: a huge reptile with feathery wings. Although its great wings flapped slowly, it moved at great speed across the city.

"Intercept!" Sweasel ordered. Despite the ban on war weapons, Security Yessers (SYs) maintained a stock of missiles to protect Babel from terrorists.

The creature on screen dropped towards the city—and disappeared. Sweasel rubbed his eyes.

"It's gone, sir," the officer confirmed.

"Dust devils and dinosaurs?!!!" Head Supervisor Sherk sputtered. The call from his lieutenant woke him —now he had to report to headquarters to give some nonsense story to his superiors. An overnight incident with no recorded evidence—why had that fool Sweasel reported it?

"Officer Bulldog at Big Dig security encountered Suspects at 0010; we monitored their movement. A VCR squad intercepted them at Desert Wild Gate but the Suspects vanished. At about same time, security monitors observed a flying reptile that also suddenly disappeared." Sweasel reviewed the facts.

"And none of our viz recorded anything!" Sherk snapped at his subordinate. "What do we have here—group hallucination?"

Joining their Security Commander, they whisked across the complex to the Command Center to meet the High Security Counselor. The Dominion took unexplained activities seriously—particularly so close to the TRI-WAC.

"Come in, gentlemen." The High Counselor sat at a large podium on a raised platform. Behind him, screens showed tense faces of Rangers Shirl and Knot, the Airspace Security Yesser, and Officer Bulldog.

"We have a Level IV Security Breach with several eyewitness accounts but no substantiating records," said the Commander.

"Yes sir. Central System went down during the altercation—which occurred between 2400 and 0630. The officer observed two youths at 0010 near Development Sector II; we monitored them for 19.8 kiloseconds." (A kilosecond, 1000 seconds, equaled 16 minutes 40 seconds in Old Time. The Dominion had switched to decimal time measurement for consistency.)

"Rangers observed suspects at Desert Wild Portal at 0600; simultaneously Air Security observed a large flying reptilian creature moving from Wild to City Center and disappearing. Although all this activity showed on our monitors, recorders are blank."

"We must contain this situation," said the Counselor, a tall dignified figure garbed in the purple robe of the Dominion. "I suspect that the Nature Heads have concocted a series of illusionary events to disrupt security in advance of the TRI-WAC. We don't know how they hacked the Central System and disabled the incident recording monitors. But we will not be intimidated.

"Ensure that all tales of flying dragons, dust devils and urban hikers are nullified. Check the Urban Tattlers Network and contain any Newswatcher accounts."

Calm face with thin lips pulled into a tight smile—the Counselor exuded the confidence of the Dominion. "Commander, your security has failed to contain a situation just prior to the TRI-WAC. An official reprimand and step demotion will be added to the personnel file of each Yesser involved in this affair."

Sherk blanched, but kept his face neutral. The Counselor's words had the force of law. He should have sent Sweasel home last night instead of telling him to handle the incident. Now the Dominion was involved. Sweasel's reprimand postponed retirement another year and set him back a grade. Worse, the dark forces that ruled the city had him on their radar. He sensed menace behind the Counselor's smooth words.

The Counselor gave a tight-lipped smile. "We will send the Nature Heads a message that terrorist tactics will not be tolerated. Accelerate park restoration and rearrange scheduling. Puddicombe Park near MERC-1102 should be expedited for emergency improvement effective this morning."

The Counselor slid back his ergo-seat and stood up. The Commander also stood.

"We will handle it, Excellency," the Commander said.

"Remain on alert, Yessers," the Counselor said. "Progress will continue and antiurban subversion will be eradicated. Be sure you are on the right side." He turned and glided out of the Command Center, a sober figure against the dawning light.

The Counselor's pod zipped towards the Citadel. His face seemed serene but his thin lips tightened slightly. He listened intently to the Voices.

"Yes," he said. "We cannot tolerate disruption. We will do what needs to be done—quietly."

"What are you doing with my files, jerk!" Lewis Watcher sputtered as the Security Yesser gently removed his wrist tab. She passed it through a small device that hummed softly. "You are violating my civil rights! How dare you mess with my files?" he asked as the uniformed SY gave him back the wrist tab.

The Yesser had come to his portal before dawn and demanded entry for Amber Security purposes. She introduced herself as Officer Mindy Muddle.

"Sorry, Mr. Watcher," said Officer Muddle. "We have evidence that radical Activists created mass illusionary events in your sector late last night. We need to confiscate all event records until after the Triannual World Administrative Convention. The illusions could create mass hysteria and launch riots aimed at disrupting the TRI-WAC. We must contain this problem.

"Your tab is intact except for last night's recordings," she added. "I will return those to you as soon as release is authorized."

She gave the old man an apologetic smile. "Sorry for the disruption, but we must protect public safety, Mr. Watcher. You can file your story on all the events, including the illusions, once the Amber Alert is rescinded."

Mr. Watcher observed as the SY joined her partner waiting outside and zoomed off for the Security Auto. "Good thing I scrambled the kids' IDs after they left," he thought, then tapped out a special alert to his virtual audience.

The Quetzalcoatlus knew exactly where to go. She dropped from the sky, stopping right in front of Caleb's place, tilting a wing for the boy to slide off, then soared up and dropped again onto the small patch of early spring grass in front of Keren's. Keren slid down the proffered wing. Quezti—as the creature called herself—dipped her huge head once and Keren heard *Go in the Keeper's care.* Then the reptile sprang into the air and disappeared.

"I see *dyno!*" a loud cry greeted her as she slipped in the door. Tug stood in the gather room, his MAR slung over his shoulder. Peering outside through the portals, he had seen the big lizard in the gleam of the outside lights.

She hugged the small boy to her chest. "Yes Tug," she whispered urgently. "Her name is Quezti. She took me on a secret mission." She figured that if Tug blabbed the truth to her parents, it would sound like one of his fantasy adventures. Never hurt to take precautions.

"Tug, the secret mission is almost complete. Remember we are Secret Agents. We cannot reveal our assignment or the mission will fail," Keren intoned.

"Mission fail..." Tug's lip quivered. "No, *not* fail. We win!" His bright eyes looked a little droopy and he struggled to stand at attention. "Await orders, Captain Keren," he announced. "Await briefing on dyno-soar mission."

"Officer Tug, return to your quarters for rest period," she whispered. "I will brief you when I return from school mission. During the day, assume normal duties. Do not draw attention from adults." Tug usually accompanied her parents to the store, where he puttered around, providing constant challenges.

They headed for their rooms. Three hours is not much sleep, Keren thought. She and Caleb would go to school as usual and see if the Keeper's promised guidance showed up.

chapter eleven
DESTRUCTION

Tug slept in. Keren dragged herself out to eat breakfast with Mother and Dad. They seemed drawn and preoccupied. "What's up?" Keren ventured.

"We're worried about what the TRI-WAC will do to art and nature in the city," Mother said.

"The last convention went very badly," Keren agreed. "That's how we got those URPs!"

"'Urban restoration program' indeed," Dad grimaced. "Just one more excuse to dismantle the last natural areas and replace them with reengineered vegetation and bioplastic plant substitutes."

"The Parks Authority claims the bioplastics are easier to maintain; they don't need water or sunlight," Keren said. "So the Dominion can build sky towers and create 'street canyons' to its heart's content. Not that it has a heart."

She flicked on Newswatch.

"In advance of TRI-WAC, the Urban Progressive Coalition (UPC) has announced its new Progress Platform." News anchor Niles Nielsen gave a smug smile. "The UPC proposes a ban on walking or cycling outside approved nature simulations, more funding for world security, and registering all Nature Heads as potential threats to urbanity."

The viz cut to a grim face of UPC president Edgar Squeeze. "It's time to put Nature Heads into the museums where they belong," he said. "No more living in the past; the future beckons. We will protect our thriving system from the retrogressives."

"But Mr. Squeeze, polls indicate that a sizeable number of Babelites like nature and favor a 'go slow' approach to urbanization." The perky reporter shoved her record tab towards Squeeze's frown. "What do you say to people who don't like your platform?"

Squeeze's sneer became a benevolent smile. "We all benefit from the Babels—from our healthy, secure, urban atmosphere." Then he glowered. "I have a message to those who stand in the path of progress, who stand against our finest accomplishments: move aside or move outside.

"Nature Heads, move to one of the Wilds, if you love them so much," Squeeze added. "There will be ample new housing after the TRI-WAC!"

News anchor Nielsen reappeared, looking grave. "Mr. Squeeze is referring to the Wild Development Protocol," he said. "The UPC, Dominationists and developers have advanced this initiative to improve Wilds worldwide."

Images flashed: a giant chalet perched on the world's highest Mountain Wild, a development of giant treehouses perched on huge dipterocarp trees of a Tropical Wild, and a chain of linked artificial islands sprouting luxurious dwellings in the midst of an Ocean Wild. "These are some of the Wild development proposals already in the planning stage," Nielsen added.

"This year's TRI-WAC could be the most significant in history— and this time next year some Babelites could be living in the Wilds! Stay tuned to Newsflash for constant coverage. It's your Convention and your future."

Newsflash moved on to the next big news: the world's bigger Babels had initiated a tower construction competition. A schematic showed Babel II 4.1's proposed entry: a soaring 1200-meter needle in the middle of Central City Park.

Dad sighed. "That must be the only place in the city with any undeveloped land," he said, and snapped off the viz. "That's enough of this drivel."

"Maybe we could be the first family to move to a Wild," Keren joked. "But I don't think the Wildlings would like it."

Mother's tab glowed, and she left the table. "That was Mr. Snark from your MERC," she said a minute later. "He knew about my search for your teacher. Dr. Dierk is taking leave until after the TRI-WAC. I imagine he is quite distressed by the Wilds Development Protocol."

"He probably needed some time away," Keren agreed. She scooted out the door.

Caleb waited at the corner. "Any new messages?" she asked.

"Not yet, I imagine we will be told when we need to know," Caleb said. He looked rested, not like he had been hiking and dancing with Wildlings all night. "It's weird, we had two encounters with authorities, but they apparently still don't know who we are. We are still undercover!"

"Have you watched Newsflash?" Keren asked as they took their favorite route behind the glide paths towards the parks. She updated him.

"Maybe that's what the Keeper meant about destructive forces?" Caleb pondered.

"Oh Cal!" Keren cried.

Puddicombe Pocket Park had vanished. Big mesquite trees lay like dying giants along the path. Huge excavators scurried, ripping up the grass, delving into the soil and piling it up along a flattened expanse. A fence netter chugged out an expanse of orange fencing to block their route.

"Sorry, kids," a worker yelled over the din. "Park Improvement Zone. You can't enter. Unsafe." He held up his wrist, and flashed the Park Improvement Order. Their virtual signboards read:

30-3-2055 PARK IMPROVEMENT ORDER

By Immediate Order of the Dominion:

Puddicombe Park, Sector I, Central City, Babylon II, is closed to all civilian entry for Park Improvement Activities (PIAs). Planned Improvements include:

- Channelization of Puddy Creek

- Removal of excessive vegetation

- Removal of hazard trees

- Installation of Gen trees

- Decorative Gen floral plantings

- Removal of Ped Path

- Installation of Auto-accessible rails and viewing Tower

PIAs will proceed for estimated 90 days

Puddicombe Park Improvement Project is one
of seven PIPs immediately initiated by this order throughout
Babylon II.4.1. Refer to link for details of other PIPs
parklandPIPs@babl.urb

This is a Construction Safety Zone. All construction
personnel must wear protective headgear and deflection
suits. Citizens violating a Safety Zone order will be
subject to arrest, possible fines & imprisonment under
City Safety Code Ordinance 20575.

The screens flashed a computerized viz of a square lined by rows of
Gen trees and artificial flowers along bright emerald green carpet turf, an
engineer's fantasy of designed open space. A final motto flashed:

The Dominion: for order, safety and utility.

Caleb's brows knit together, his teeth clenched. "Payback and
intimidation," he spat out, as they turned away from the defiled sanctuary.

"The Park Improvement Plan proposed all this," Keren said. "They
just decided to implement it here first—in our favorite park."

"They may not know who we are," Caleb said. "But they know where
we live."

chapter twelve
PROPHETESS

"I bet the Central System went down again last night," Keren said as they trudged through the MERC entrance.

"Thank the Keeper for small glitches," Caleb said. "The Dominion's perfect plans always have some flaw they try to cover up."

"How are we accomplishing the Keeper's plan by just going back to school?" said Keren. "Only two school days until TRI-WAC delegates depart."

"The Keeper told us," Caleb reminded. "'Return to school and you will be shown what to do.'" He stopped and surveyed the quad in front of the MERC. "This doesn't look like a normal school day."

Several adults lounged around the quad, dressed in conspicuously neutral garb, and eyeing students filing through the front entrance. YIPs (Yessers In Plainclothes), Keren thought. Two looked at their wrist tabs—no doubt beaming screening devices to check for weapons or unusual electronics. Good thing they can't scan minds. Caleb (who could) smiled.

They took the Tred up to the 4th level OA Biology class, joining their colleagues. Cynthia and Irving looked worried.

"Wednesday was fizz," Cynthia whispered. "Mincer and her pseudoscience projects wasted most of the morning. We worked in a little 'virtch' while she babbled on, no scores. We need air time to concentrate."

"Made progress last night," Irving added. "How about you guys?"

Keren gave her best Mona Lisa smile. Long story. How would her teammates react?

They filed into the classroom and gave a collective sigh.

Ms. Mincer flounced to the front. "Class, the Triannual World Administrative Convention will commence in three days!" she gushed. "Today, we will attend a special MERC-Wide Assembly starting at 0830. OA Biology class will proceed to Assembly Auditorium via Tred 17."

Keren hated the big Treds that efficiently moved 20,000 students for assemblies, emergencies and other mass events. Although the moving bands reached speeds of 2 km/ks, a little faster than walk speed, she always squirmed with impatience as the Tred stopped for a class to slowly process aboard, slowly accelerated, then stopped again.

The assembly would feature a speaker from Citadel Policy Analysis Institute, to explain proposed Directives and their impact on urbanity. Third period classes would feature guided discussions on merits and implications.

Blah blah blah, thought Keren. Dominion propaganda and promotion thinly disguised as "education" and "civil discourse." She expected high-tech special effects; the Dominion spent a fortune on glitzy "bells and whistles" to impress young minds. Cynthia and Irving would be scoping out programming specs. With any luck they would "tweak" the programs for more interesting "special effects."

They programmed wrist tabs for note mode, picked up water sippers and filed onto the Tred, which made its start/stop progress across the huge indoor campus to Row 17 in the cavernous Assembly Auditorium. No one chattered on the Tred ride—everyone was preoccupied and worried about Dr. Dierk. Keren had new information and hope—but no idea when she could share it in this controlled environment.

On the performance platform, Snark sat with other MERC administrators. Head Administrator Dr. Woggle slowly walked to the podium.

"Middle scholars, distinguished faculty, special guests, we stand on the edge of a new era for urbanity. In three days, the Triannual World Administrative Convention will commence. Previous Conventions represent concord of 200 nations in unanimously passing directives to spread prospering Babels across the earth. This is cause for celebration."

Virtual fireworks erupted in the air around the Administrator and the amplifiers roared with prerecorded cheers while the live students applauded politely.

"It is difficult for young people to grasp the import of these Conventions. For you, the peace and prosperity of urbanity is just a way of life," Dr. Woggle continued. "But we who have lived through the chaos and disruptions of earlier eras stand in awe of what the human race has achieved in economic advancement and urbanization."

Dr. Woggle now stood in a virtual shantytown on a narrow street lined with piles of garbage. Skinny children surrounded him. The image shattered, then reassembled as backdrop images of gleaming towers, green factory farms and orderly crowds of peoples soaring on spiraling Autos. Neat, crisp, and clean.

"To outline the next urban improvement directives, I introduce Dr. Prosperity Perkins, Global Lead Analyst from the National Policy Institute of Babel II."

Dr. Perkins did not fit the grey ghost image of a GLAP (Global Lead Analyst of Policy). The tall woman strode to the podium, and fixed her intense gaze on the student audience. Young, beautiful and suited in powder blue, she exuded energy and warmth; her eyes somehow met the gaze of every audience member. She spoke in compelling tones.

Keren heard the woman's descriptions of WAC members and proposed policy directives; she saw appropriate virtual visuals filling the air. But a different message spoke in her mind.

Keren, beloved of the Keeper, you will visit many Wilds and commission Our Wildlings. At the appointed time, those you send will carry Our ways into the cities surrounding the Wilds.

Behind the well-tailored form of Dr. Perkins, Keren glimpsed the shell of Tortoise, wisdom of the Keeper. The briefing continued.

Be prepared tonight at 2300. Transportation will come to your home.

Up on the housetop, click, click, click? Keren's irreverent thought evoked a smile from Dr. Perkins. The silent conversation went both ways.

Our emissaries will not come "down through the chimney," beloved; they will arrive in your room and provide your Way, Dr. Perkins responded. *This afternoon, study and select your Wilds. Be glad, the Keeper is with you always.*

Beautiful eyes met Keren's, and she glimpsed wrinkled lids as blue eyes merged into yellow. One eyelid closed in a wink.

Keren looked around. Glazed expressions characterized most attendees but OA Biology faces lit up with surprise. Looks of alarm and then concentration crossed the faces of Caleb, Irving, Cynthia, Timmie, Sal, Bopha and others nearby. Did they each hear a personal message?

A different message—for those who hear, Keren thought.

After the assembly, they all tredded to their next class. Keren sighed when her OA English teacher tabbed out the TRI-WAC policy questions.

"So class, any immediate reactions to the TRI-WAC proposals?" Ms. Freedom asked.

Keren spoke up. "Ms. Freedom, how can the UPC push a platform through the TRI-WAC that effectively dismantles civil rights of anyone who prefers nature to urbanization? Doesn't that violate the Code of Freedoms?"

Paul Wonk added a long diatribe on civil rights defects of the UPC Progress Platform. As soon as he paused for breath, Chester Noblitts jumped in, defending urban growth, and the class debate began. Keren tried to smile attentively as her mind wandered back to her encounter with the assembly speaker. Dr. Perkins must be the Prophetess. What did she tell the others?

Her wrist tab flashed. Glancing away from the lively discussion, she saw individual images of OA Biology members blending into a group. Irving had called an assembly using the VAA (virtual assembly app). This simulated a videoconference; participants appeared to share a room. Keren enjoyed Irving's depiction of a lavish corporate conference room with a big oval table, plush chairs and a staggering thirtieth-story picture window view of Babel II 4.1 sprawling out towards the Desert Wild.

Thanks to Irving's creative tech skills, each participant appeared to "speak" as he or she texted a report. Keren could listen with one ear to her English class discussion while following the more important conversation on her screen.

Sal, Arana and I are going to rescue Dr. Dierk, Caleb messaged. *We're going to the Citadel tonight. We leave at 2300 hours—from our homes—and assemble somehow.*

Cynthia and I are providing security support Irving wrote. *The, the lady, the uh—Dr. Perkins gave Cynthia code for the Citadel Security System.*

We're gonna disable security functions and engineer virtual distractions so you can find Dr. D. without getting blasted.

She is the Prophetess Keren tabbed in. *Cal and I heard about her last night—we went to Desert Wild and met the Keeper. We'll fill you guys in at Nutri-Break. My assignment is to go to several Wilds and ask Wildlings to come to the Babels at a specified time.*

You're not going alone; I'm going with you, Bopha addressed Keren. *Can't wait.*

That made sense. The other budding biologist, Bopha, had earned the nickname "Herp" for her love of snakes.

Keren approved of the assignments for Dr. Dierk's rescue team. Arana, a lithe rock gymnast with a knack for exploring forbidden spaces, had barely missed suspension after her investigation of the MERC "crawl space" had triggered an untimely light show during the Annual Exams. Sal was a quick-witted track runner who excelled at spy simulation, and of course, Caleb was the fastest runner in MERC 1102. Keren felt a bit wistful. She wanted to join Caleb's adventure. But the Keeper's workforce had to expand.

The Prophetess had asked the rest of the class to continue simulator enhancement work, and provided them a new virtual channel unknown to Yesser monitors.

At Nutri-Break, Caleb tried to describe their meetup with the Keeper and feast with the Wildlings.

"Coordinated Cal, promenading with a Panther?" Lizzie rolled her eyes. "I'm surprised you didn't trip over Her tail."

"Suspend disbelief," Caleb said. Besides the amazing feast and Great Dance, their classmates expressed surprise that Caleb and Keren had walked across the city, met with the Keeper and Wildlings, and returned home before morning dawned.

"The Keeper can expand time as needed," Keren argued. "Wait until you experience it; then you will know. If I can believe it, anyone can."

Her words brought laughter around the dining platform where the biology classmates had crowded together. They knew Keren prided herself on her logic.

"I am wondering if someone had to go to the Wild so the Keeper could gain access here in Babel II," said Sal. "You said the Keeper isn't heard when people stop believing."

"S/HE did say something about honoring people's choices; that's why there is little sign of the Keeper in Babel II," Caleb agreed. "But I guess S/HE can be anywhere people ask."

"Sort of like a genie?" quipped Lizzie.

"Not quite; I think the Keeper gives the orders, not vice-versa!" Caleb said. "But humankind has always wanted the Keeper to be a genie. No wonder religions are so weird."

"Your wish is my command," Lizzie offered an obeisance.

"Enough philosophy; we have work," Bopha said.

"Along with the distraction of school," said Lizzie. "We'll manage work around those annoyances—virtually!"

Throughout the late morning, Keren and Bopha kept in remote contact as they reviewed Great Wilds of the World, fauna and climate. Their transport would decide the route, but they would choose Wilds and Wildlings close enough to the Babels for a recruitment visit.

Your Keeper leaves a lot of the details to us, Bopha tabbed in.

We're the biologists, Keren snapped back and then felt silly. True, she and Bopha knew a lot about the Wilds flora and fauna. But the Keeper made it all.

I guess S/HE trusts us, she tapped.

Observing a puzzled frown from her math teacher, she quickly flipped her screen back to the geometry problem. Why do I have to "prove" these triangles are congruent? Why?

She sighed and refocused on the proof.

chapter thirteen
DARK FORCES

D
r. Dierk looked up from the reading screen and stretched along the ergo chair. His modest quarters included comp system access (one way) so he could continue Wilds cataloguing research and lecture prep, a walking band with simulator, rest platform, meal platform and seat, and even a small "writing desk." An outside window offered views of Desert Wilds foothills across the megacity. The Security Yessers offered no punishment—just caution. They wanted to contain potential "subversive elements" prior to the TRI-WAC. They saw it as containment, not punishment. Dierk disagreed. He felt caged and frustrated.

He sprang to his feet at the soft knock on his door. "Yes? Come in!"

The Counselor glided into the room, a serene and slender figure. He smiled.

"Greetings, High Counselor Dred. To what do I owe this unexpected pleasure of your visit?" Dierk asked. "And how long does the Dominion plan to illegally confine me with no charges?"

"Only until the TRI-WAC begins, Dr. Dierk. It's for your protection. Key informers have associated you with a seditious plot to disrupt the TRI-WAC, and claim the high-powered simulator allocated to your lab for research has been reprogrammed to send subversive messages. Rather than prosecute these serious charges, and possibly terminate your promising career, the Dominion decided to isolate you until this window of danger closes.

"I am sure you know that we have the authority to maintain public safety and security," Dred added. Amber eyes met mild blue as the two men faced each other.

"Peace at what price, Dred?" Dierk met his stare—and saw an unfathomable abyss in the yellow orbs. The eyes matched the gold stare of a mountain lion but had no spark of life. *What am I dealing with?* He felt no fear, only emptiness.

"Believe me, Dr. Dierk. There are forces you do not want to unleash. The Dominion has been charged with keeping the peace; if we do not, they will."

Dierk blanched. He had always suspected this. Such forces explained why perfectly reasonable people in the education system would water down controversial but well-known facts after a letter or a visit from some Dominion representative, the raw destructiveness behind development projects, trees and vegetation shredded and urban wildlife eradicated, the darkness that pervaded public agreement on urban expansion and economic growth, and the terror he sensed in Yessers within his own profession.

"Why should I fear these forces, Dred?" he asked. "They have no power over me."

"They will harm anyone who opposes them," Dred said.

Did he glimpse fear in those tawny eyes?

"We are concerned that your young OA protégés will try something foolish in your absence—and come up against something that could do them harm," said Dred. "I am pleading with you to cooperate. To fully outline your plans and identify your collaborators—so we can protect them until the danger passes."

"Why don't you arrest and confine all my students?" Dierk suggested. "Perhaps I've brainwashed them all to love and fight for the Wilds."

"We have no evidence or information on any student. Our Tattlers indicate normal education activities at your MERC. Your students are attending classes and assemblies, carrying out assignments, continuing normal routines except..." Dred hesitated.

"Two young people from your MERC sector and age group of your classes were observed walking across the entire western sector last night," Dred added. "Security tracked their route but identities are still unknown.

"The suspects illegally entered the Desert Wild early this morning and somehow eluded an entire Ranger interception team at the entrance," Dred said. "A search turned up no sign of human visitation. No students are absent from the MERC 1102 OA program today—other than 23 excused absences due to illness which checked out as legitimate. I want to find out the identities of these two students—and what they did in the Desert Wild."

"Why don't you have IDs?" Dr. Dierk asked.

"Central System went down last night; overloaded from security preparations," Dred said.

Dierk collected his thoughts. "How would I know about this?" he asked. "I have been confined during this altercation. DHS confiscated my tab and redirected my comp. I last saw my students in the OA

Biology classroom Wednesday before my arrest. How would I be in contact with them?"

Again the empty eyes met his. "Dr. Dierk, help us. Many lives may be at stake."

"Sorry, I can't help you," Dierk responded. *Particularly with the choices you have made, and the consequences.*

Abruptly, the Counselor turned on his heel and motioned to the door. It slid open. Dierk considered a run for the door. "Don't," Dred said.

Dierk's involuntary shift towards the tall figure froze. He could not move. *Power indeed.*

"Do let me know if new information comes to you, Dr. Dierk," Counselor Dred said. "Your tab is programmed for direct access to me."

And no one else, Dierk thought as the counselor glided out and the door slid shut behind him. The temporary paralysis ended. *What got hold of me?*

Whatever it was, it had a cruel hold on High Security Counselor Narlor Dred.

"Pleeeeease...," Dred pleaded. "He knows nothing, he cannot help us. The Enemy is working but we are monitoring all Their helpers. They cannot move without our knowing. They cannot stop your Great Urban Expansion. You will rule. Urbanity wishes it. Humanity craves it."

Alone in his Auto pod, the Counselor screamed silently. He held his throbbing head in his hands, wracked with pain and chaotic visions.

Terrible teeth bit, venomous insects stung, fire burned, horrifying creatures ripped and tore at the neurons in his brain—all unseen, only imagined. But the pain and terror felt very real.

There is only destruction for those who fail Us. Taste the power of your Master. Do not fail again.

The Auto came to a stop and Dred stepped off. A Yesser hurried up. "Your Eminence, welcome back to the Counsel Hall. Your sector briefing is prepared."

The Counselor smiled down at the assistant. "Drudge, change in plans. Arrange a security visit to MERC 1102 sector; inform the administration that a contingent from the Dominion's Central Security Authority will arrive at 1500. Tell Snark to arrange a briefing from the Level III OA Biology class students."

The assistant's eyes widened slightly. "Briefing from students?"

"The Security Council needs to be fully aware of any activities affecting the Wilds," Dred said. "Tell Snark we expect OA class to explain the Wilds visitation and simulation project Dr. Dierk has been overseeing. We will include other personnel in this briefing," he added. "The Head Ranger and the Visitor Control Lead Ranger from the Desert Wild and Officer Bulldog from Sector V. Ensure their transport to our facility ASAP. I need to meet with them before our MERC visit."

Always meticulous, Drudge acknowledged with a brief nod, turned and went to make it so.

Dred smiled tightly. Once they identified suspects, interrogation could begin. But it must be finessed. The public loved OA students and thought juvenile rights sacrosanct. To charge students with violating the Wilds visit moratorium would be admitting a Wilds visit had occurred, which the Dominion had not acknowledged. Security breaches reduced public confidence and raised public anxiety. Fearmongering could be helpful, but not prior to the TRI-WAC, meticulously designed to inspire public confidence.

I will handle it he affirmed.

chapter fourteen
THE INVESTIGATION

"**A**LL OA BIOLOGY STUDENTS FROM DR. DIERK'S SECTION PLEASE REPORT IMMEDIATELY TO THE CENTRAL ADMINISTRATOR'S COMPLEX."

What??? Keren looked at the speakers in disbelief. The announcement repeated.

Not that she minded an excuse to miss Fifth Period Phys Ed...but... *are we in trouble? What's wrong?* She looked around at the gym full of preadolescent girls decked out in sports tunics. The three games of volleyball had stopped. Everyone stared at her and the two other OA Bio students.

Ms. Kristen, an ex-pro soccer player more comfortable in the PE uniform than her skirt-top civvies, gave her a funny look. "OA students dismissed," she said. "Take the CAC Tred."

"They said 'immediately,'" Kristen added. "Just go as is." Yuck. Unshowered in shorts. How undignified.

Keren, Cynthia and Bopha broke ranks and headed for the locker room.

They caught the Central Administration Complex (CAC) Tred. Keren flushed with embarrassment as they merged into a line of suited Yessers holding small hand cases—drones headed for the hive. Students didn't take this transport, unless they were in trouble.

The gleaming white Dome of Knowledge appeared ahead, soaring above the CAC mini-campus. The Tred slowed to a stop at the entrance, which was flanked by statues of great scholars: DaVinci, Newton, Einstein. The river of Yessers flowed off the Tred and split in various directions.

The OA Biology students reunited in the entrance hall, gazing up at sky blue cathedral ceilings. Perhaps there should be a painting of a scholar touching the finger of another human scholar, Keren thought. The hall looked like a place of worship.

They deactivated their tabs and huddled. No records for the sensors. They eyed each other nervously. "What are you in for?" Caleb asked, releasing a little laughter.

"Sent to the principal's office *again*," quipped Lizzie with an expressive sigh.

"Welcome, Over Achievers." Mr. Snark hurried across the hall towards the wary students. "Thank you for getting here so promptly. We have very important visitors."

The ceiling parted above them. With a soft hum, an air transport slowly descended and rested its bulk on a landing pad in the center of the entrance hall. Six people stepped out.

They recognized High Counselor Dred from news images, along with the Desert Wild Head Ranger in her dress greens. Two high level Yessers flanked the officials, followed by two men Keren recognized: the jowly faced Security Yesser who hassled them at the Big Dig site, and the Ranger who met them at the Desert Wild entrance just before dawn.

The Counselor motioned the Ranger and Yesser to his side and spoke to them quietly. The two witnesses began carefully scrutinizing the huddle of students standing before them.

Keren waited in horror, expecting recognition, her mind numb with apprehension. *Caught?*

Deputy Administrator Snark broke the uncomfortable silence. "OA Biology classmates, please welcome High Counselor Dred from the Dominion and Head Ranger Shirl from the Desert Wild. Their Eminences are sorry to disrupt your schoolwork but have high security business. His Eminence High Counselor Dred," he intoned.

The Counselor smiled at the apprehensive students as his hirelings carefully appraised each face. "Peace and security, young scholars," he said. "The TRI-WAC will convene Sunday. For security reasons, the Dominion has banned Wild visits.

"Early this morning, two middle-grade students illegally entered the Desert Wild. We suspect these trespassers came from your class."

At the collective gasp, Dred raised his hands peaceably. "Do not fear. We do not plan to press charges against the perpetrators. The Dominion esteems young scholars and recognizes your passion for the Wilds. But we need to understand the motive behind this violation."

The students looked at each other. An illegal Wilds visit might be the least of their offenses.

"We have two witnesses who will identify the perpetrators," Dred said.

Keren kept her face neutral as the ranger continued to look over the students. To her surprise, the man scanned her briefly, then Caleb, with no glimmer of recognition. He continued his inspection of the other OA students. The Security Yesser also surveyed the group, his face wrinkled in puzzlement.

Keren heard the calm voice of the Prophetess. *Just as these ones refuse to know truth, so they will not see and not hear.* Could the Keeper make their faces unrecognizable? How?

The Counselor leaned down and conferred with his witnesses. After head shaking and frowns, Dred summoned Mr. Snark. They spoke in hushed tones.

"OA Biology students, proceed to alcove 1A and take a seat," Mr. Snark said. "Our visitors need a closer examination."

The uncomfortable students trooped past the administrator into the room where ergo chairs lined a table. They sat down. No one touched a tab. Keren heard Caleb's reassuring voice on a different channel. *Do not fear. We are protected. They cannot see or understand. Be still and wait.* From the relieved expressions around the table, everyone got the message.

The dignitaries sat at a small platform by the door. At Snark's signal, one student at a time came up and sat in front of the platform. Each met with Counselor Dred while his subordinates carefully scanned the student. After the interrogation, Dred dismissed each student to return to class.

Keren watched Lizzie laugh and toss her head at a remark from the High Counselor. She worried about her "turn." Then she realized she could still mentally communicate with Bopha, although neither spoke and they sat at opposite ends of the big table. They continued planning the Wilds visit and discussed key Wildlings to meet.

Everyone returned to virtual planning, communicating even with their tabs off. A new communication channel had opened. Behind their placid disinterested faces, discussions continued. Apprehension and boredom became quiet progress.

Beneath his rigid demeanor, Ranger Knot felt waves of frustration. He observed facial features, expressions, body type and movements of each student who conversed with the Counselor. With 20 years of training on witness identification, he could detect lies and evasion and often identified a criminal through an unguarded smile or twitch. He had engraved in his memory the faces of the two miscreants who eluded his force this morning. In his mind he saw the tall gangly youth and the intensely focused girl.

Yet he did not see them among this group of suspects. He scanned the animated blonde joking with Counselor Dred. Not his serious morning visitor.

"Next student, please."

Knot could not fail again. A whole VCR containment force knocked flat by a dust devil. No sign of the visitors in the Desert Wild. He could not bungle this test before the highest security official in Babel II 4.1. "Focus, Knot," he told himself.

Officer Bulldog felt frustrated. He had given those kids a good look, even scanned their faces, yet neither his recorder nor memory helped find them here.

"Caleb Benson," Snark read, and looked up as the tall youth left his seat and arranged his long frame in the chair before the platform.

Caleb shot an amused glance at Mr. Snark, who must long to know the reason for this unprecedented visit by the High Counselor to a MERC. He played his role as host and facilitator, presenting each student, then returning to his seat at the far side of the platform, seeming to strain to hear the conversations. Caleb knew that Dr. Dierk's Wilds field trips had brought honors to the MERC 1102 OA Program. But now this work had attracted the Dominion—risky. And Snark had no idea about the new Wilds work.

Caleb felt relaxed as he faced a Dominion official intent on stopping his mission. He knew that the Ranger and Security Yesser scrutinizing his features saw someone different. *Who do I look like?* He could sense their frustration and sent them a sense of calm. He felt them relax.

Dred smiled with no kindness in his eyes, only a fathomless depth. Caleb looked into an eternity he had not seen before, something dark and threatening. He reached for the human mind behind the eyes and did not find it—instead a dark fearsome presence joined his thoughts and began to search him. He drew back immediately and felt a safer, reassuring Presence surrounding him. The Name is a strong tower; the righteous runs into it and is safe, he thought as the Counselor addressed him.

"Mr. Benson, you won the Inter-MERC Cross Country Competition for Level III this year. Congratulations." Dred's smile did not meet his yellow eyes. "You are a rarity: a young man who prefers walking to the Auto."

"Thank you, sir. I like to walk," Caleb agreed, holding the Presence strong around him, wondering if the Counselor's inner powers read him. A stalemate?

"You, young man, could walk across the western end of Babel II 4.1 in a few hours," Dred said. "Did you leave your home last night, walk across the city with a female student, and enter the Desert Wild entrance at 0600 this morning?"

A direct question. Now what? The ranger and guard looked like predators staring down their prey, not recognizing him but sensing his discomfort. "I diii..." A deafening sound shook the dome and cut off Caleb's reluctant reply. An earthquake?

Dred's wrist tab flashed red. "What?" the High Counselor turned away. His face darkened as he tilted his ear towards the tumble of voices from his wrist. He jumped to his feet and swept out of the room. Mr. Snark, hurrying after him, received a curt order and returned.

"Students, please remain while the High Counselor attends to the emergency. We will finish as soon as possible," Snark told them. "You may use your tabs to resume class assignments."

"I can't play volleyball with my tab—guess I could run a sim," Keren whispered to Caleb as he returned to the table. He met her eyes but didn't smile, too shaken by his encounter with Counselor Dred.

"Toasted, I thought. He asked me a direct question and...well, I never lie. Not directly. I don't know how to make stuff up," Caleb said, eliciting knowing smiles around the table. Everyone knew about his truth policy. "But why did the Counselor run out?"

Cynthia Cyber grinned. "A security drone miscalculated its path and flew low over the MERC; I guess its sound waves damaged the Dome of

Knowledge," she reported. "I imagine the Counselor is trying to deal with the PR fallout! Doesn't look good for the Dominion."

"What amazing timing!" Caleb said.

"Not totally a coincidence," Irving chimed in. "Cyn and I got a message that you had trouble up there and we needed to help. We had just developed a SAT intercept, and I noticed a security drone in the vicinity and...pretty easy to engineer a little elevation drop."

No one asked who sent the message.

Temporarily freed from adult scrutiny, the students discussed their interview experiences in whispers.

"I found myself really calm and wonderfully forgetful about our work, vague like a dream I had," Lizzie said. "I joked around with the Counselor, never got to the subject."

"I think I bored him explaining the statutory basis for Wilds protection, and why the Wilds Development Protocol is violation of legislative precedent," Paul Wonk said.

"He saw me as prime suspect," said Arana. "He knew all about my UrbEX adventures through the towers of Babel—but I told him I do my adventuring inside, not outside. I knew nothing about last night's escapade. Other than what you told me, and I couldn't remember that."

"Sounds like the Counselor bored-in on Caleb," Paul said. "And Keren is up next."

"Maybe we need to develop a Drone drop app for emergencies," Lizzie suggested with a giggle.

"I'm glad you young people are enjoying yourselves." Snark appeared at the table. "Let's resume the interviews. Ms. Anderson."

Somehow Caleb had been cleared. But how would Keren survive?

Keren's interview went quickly, if not smoothly. The Counselor appeared shaken by the embarrassing security flub. For her part, Keren felt awful meeting a suited High Official in her gym tunic.

"No need for embarrassment, Ms. Anderson." The yellow eyes held amusement. "I understand you came directly from Phys Ed." Dred consulted his tab. "Your parents own an art supply store, and are involved with the Nature Head movement, Ms. Anderson. You walk to school with Mr. Benson."

She nodded. His point?

"Your class discussed the Wilds Development Protocol slated for TRI-WAC enactment." Amber eyes bored into hers. "You have written articles on the importance of rare fauna in the Wilds. What do you think about the Protocol?"

"Do I think the Protocol will impact Wildlings survival and habitat?" Keren answered. "A directive that declassifies protected areas will reduce and fragment habitat, destroying most of the diverse fauna on this small planet, fauna that may be key to supporting life. Why is the Dominion so intent on destroying the natural and wild on this planet?" The bold question coming out of her mouth surprised her.

"Ms. Anderson, my life's work is protecting security and prosperity," Dred snapped. "Urbanity has provided more accord and more peace than all the fledgling, half-hearted efforts to 'preserve nature' ever could. What I fear is a return to anarchy and self-interest. You are too young to remember a world of warfare and loss. I am not."

The Counselor's face darkened and he blinked rapidly. Beside him, the Ranger and Yesser stared blankly. Dred regained control. "Return to class, Ms. Anderson."

The remaining interviews went quickly; Knot and Bulldog did not recognize any student. Flustered by the drone strike and angered at his incompetent security forces, Dred lost his cool unnerving style. Students did not seem intimidated or flummoxed; some even confronted him about Dr. Dierk's disappearance and the legality of Wilds development. None showed any direct knowledge of the Desert Wild visit.

Dred had taken a gamble spending personal time on the venture; he felt rage at the poor performance of his subordinates and his own loss of control. He gained only the unsurprising information that Dr. Dierk's students represented a pool of opposition to urban progress and Wilds declassification. Though young and powerless, they warranted continued observation.

Not enough, Dred, the dark Voices warned as the visitation party lifted off from the MERC in strained silence. He felt the terror and shame of his subordinates, who no doubt realized their failure and feared the consequences. The air in the transport vehicle felt thick as a black cloud of smoke, heavy with malevolence and terror.

chapter fifteen
DISCIPLINE

S hirl and Knot sat side by side on a small platform outside the Chamber of Discipline. It's not fair, Shirl thought. I never saw these interlopers, I never dealt with them, and now because of staff incompetence, I lose everything I worked for! Only the Powers know if I can get out of this alive. Senior Executive Yessers took full responsibility for any failures on their watch. They served at the pleasure of the Dominion; achieving high rank meant signing away all personal rights.

Shirl checked her reflection on her tab's personal vanity app. She would walk into this composed and professional, although she might not leave the same way.

She glanced at her subordinate. Knot baffled her. His Service-wide cred in Visitor Control made him a perfect fit for the Desert Wild post. But he lost it over a natural disturbance and a couple of kids—then his famous photographic memory failed at the most crucial time in the history of the Service. She frowned. He looked calm and composed, almost relieved. Strange guy.

The entrance slid open and Officer Bulldog staggered out. His face contorted, and he cried like a small boy. Two Security Yessers held the guard's arms. "Come on grandpa," one sneered. "We have a place for you at the Eastside Elderly Assistance Center. You can't take care of yourself anymore."

A deep voice spoke from the chamber. "Head Ranger Shirl, enter." The head ranger stood up and stepped into the darkness.

She could barely make out the disciplinary specialist (DS) in black uniform and face mask. Impersonal discipline contributed to the intimidation factor. A white-jacketed medical professional also stood by. Shirl knew the medic would monitor vital signs and intervene to ensure no one terminated directly under the procedure. Capital punishment had been outlawed years ago.

The DS motioned to the simulator. The recliner seat had restraints. Shirl sat, trying not to wince as the DS attached sensors and tightened the bands.

"Head Ranger Shirl, for dereliction of duties to protect a Wild under your charge and to enforce a directive, you have received a career downgrade. In addition, to demonstrate the gravity of failing the Dominion in a High Security Situation—you have been sentenced to simulated death."

The medic moved in and gently placed a little cap on her head. "One moment, please. We need a brain scan to determine the appropriate discipline." Shirl heard a little humming, and knew that invisible rays scrutinized the contents of her cranial amygdalae. The humming stopped and she waited.

Shirl repressed a cry as her surroundings merged into a wet, humid, overwhelming landscape—a dark jungle of vines, shrubs and trees covered with lichens and moss. Lost in a wet tropical Wild with no survival pack, no protective gear. She slapped at her legs, feeling the tiny bites of countless mosquitos; her eye was swelling from a bee sting. In disgust, she pulled at a leech attached to her thigh. The incessant heat crawled inside her and sweat poured down her face.

A roar shook the ground, and Shirl forgot about her tiny torments as soft paws moved towards her. She turned to run and tripped over a vine, slamming her head on a hard root. She struggled, grappling through the tangled vines, shoving through slippery ferns as the beast gained on her. She felt the crushing weight on her back and sharp teeth on her neck searching for her jugular...the fangs bit deep, pulled chunks from her body, devoured her alive.

The DS and MD watched as the well-dressed official struggled against the restraints, tears streaming from closed eyes, mouth open in a silent scream, enhancers running down her sweaty face. "20 seconds," the MD noted.

"New record," the DS said. He had won the bet. Top people lost it quicker in the Worst Fears Simulator.

The DS looked forward to working with Ranger Knot. A tough character—jungle terrors would not faze him. Although the MD insisted a long-hidden childhood terror would emerge as the best discipline, the DS had a feeling Knot feared crowds. They would soon find out.

Sitting in his ergo-chair, Dred half attended the droning voice of the Babel II 4.1 chief security engineer outlining precautions for containing protests and ensuring delegate safety. He glanced at his tab, tuned to the proceedings in the Chamber of Discipline where Ranger Shirl immediately lost all elements of her highly cultivated professional image. He doubted that Knot would crack so quickly.

Other disciplinary procedures followed the Central System breakdown, monitor failure and drone drop above MERC 1102. Responsible parties had been rounded up and their discipline initiated. No deaths, but a number of key officials would have to be replaced, as they would be mentally unfit after extreme simulator discipline.

Dred ranked too high for a chamber of discipline. His Terrors carried out his punishment within his head. Hornets and wasps had stung his brain since the transport left MERC 1102. With each jolt came the hissed *Failure! Failure!* and a feeling of brain cell connections ripping apart. Not real, he reminded himself, but the pain persisted.

I am essential to Your work, he countered against the blinding, shredding forces inside his head. *You cannot disembody me. You need me.*

The Powers dealt directly with Dred, as security played a key role in their strategies. He did not know if his fellow Counselors had such access and such terror—no one ever discussed these matters. He sometimes caught a flash of insight or fear in the eyes of his peers that indicated something similar. He did not ponder it; speculation enraged those who had access to all of his faculties. He already knew their rage.

The stinging pains subsided. They had accepted his argument—or they had refocused on pockets of suffering in the discipline chambers throughout the Dominion offices. Dred considered disciplinary use of simulation as the acme of his career. Urbanity no longer inflicted physical torture or death on miscreants. But the mental anguish from simulated fear offered a gift that kept on giving. The incredible mental processes of the human psyche, once incited, became ongoing personalized instruments of torture.

Posttraumatic stress disorder, Dred thought. And we can create it.

And this gift I gave to You, Dred pointed out to his Superiors. *Our technology, our science, and our gifts for solving our problems have become Your finest tool for destruction—from the inside out.*

As it has always been, the Voices agreed. *Your kind has the ability to adapt—and you offer it to Us for our work. Clubs to kill Wildlings—and each other. Fire to warm—and destroy. Dams to control—and decimate—the waters and land. Fueling your civilization—and altering the atmosphere. And now, altering the human mind.*

You need me, Dred said. *You cannot work alone.*

We need humans for work, They agreed. *And so does the Adversary. Continue to help Them and fail Us, and you will join Us in disembodiment long before your scheduled time.*

A sharp stab behind the eyes and the presence left. Dred raised a hand at the Security Yesser.

"Your security measures assume neutral conditions," Dred snapped. "High Amber Alert is *not* neutral!" The engineer stopped mid-word and tried to regain his composure.

"Security Commander Frost. What are the steps of our preemptive strategy?" Dred asked.

"We have an unresolved Level V Security Situation: illegal Wilds entry, unidentified trespassers and an apparent conspiracy to disrupt the TRI-WAC with the perpetrators yet to be identified."

Commander Frost stood, motioning the security engineer back to his seat. He shifted the display on the room monitor to a schematic diagram of Babel II 4.1 and its defense ports.

"We have initiated Level V precautions: mandatory curfew at 2100 hours for all residents and shutdown of intercity travel except for official business over next 36 hours. This will protect the launch of all delegate transport," Frost said. "Civic warning scheduled for 1600 hours.

"Green and Nature Head groups have registered protest events for Thursday evening and Saturday. Urban Peace-making Forces are assigned to monitor and terminate any threats. Undercover security is monitoring Central Sector around MERC 1102. Inter-tab virtual database has been enhanced to pinpoint any system disruption."

Dred knew Frost had made up the detailed report on the spot, creating design visuals from his tab as he moved through the points.

The Counselor smiled. Yessers anticipated poorly but reacted to the past with excellence. If forced to create a plan, they would carry it out to exacting detail. His underlings did not understand the threat they faced, but they had the resources to contain it.

Not only Yessers had suffered for failing to find the pro-Wilds conspirators. In a place as real as the backstage is to a theater production, the true Rulers of Babel II screamed with pain and terror only the unfleshed could experience. As beings totally composed of energy, their essence had become chaotic raging pain. Their Energizer who had derived power from the original Source of all Life had long practice in distorting and disrupting the life force of those who served it.

When it usurped Life, the Energizer lost its personality. As the ultimate impersonal force, the unPerson, it devoted itself to destruction. Its followers thrived on derived power, a dark energy that flowed through them while undoing works of life. But today that dark energy flowed in toxic torrents; the Powers screamed silently and died a thousand un-deaths. If they could be seen, they would appear as black clouds of smoke twisting and contorting.

Taste the Abyss, the Voice raged around them, shaking a realm limitless, yet separate from the physical world.

Many have been destroyed today, Your Darkness, protested the highest ranked spirit in the Babel II 4.1 Outpost, Counselor Dred's handler.

Yessss, many. The wrong ones! the Voice shrieked, sending the clouds tumbling and colliding. *Where are Our victims among the Adversary's forces? Nowhere! Not one! Not one hurt! Not one destroyed! Not even one frightened! Are you serving the Keeper?!* It spat out the word with disgust.

For endless eons the spirits screamed and buzzed in torment; they had no sense of time or its limits. Their existence focused on the physical world where they spied on, deceived, and directed their human agents—the best force for destruction. They lived in boredom when humans slept or ignored their advances, and in these rare times of discipline, in utter terror.

This elite group of dark forces rarely failed. All had scratched and clawed their way to the top rank of Babel II 4.1—the flagship city of urbanity, the Energizer's finest achievement in human history. The Energizer claimed the Babels as success—having neatly knit together human desires for peace and prosperity, idealistic beliefs and engineering skills into soaring towers and clean, antiseptic urban centers.

Our time comes, the spirits reminded their Master. All traces of despicable "natural" life—flora and fauna—would be erased and supplanted by human-engineered substitutes, manageable, predictable, clean. *Only the microbial kingdom remains—and our human engineers will soon resolve that problem.*

Our time comes, one spirit repeated, trying to calm the waves of dark malice from the infuriated Energizer. *None of Their subjects can stop this.*

Soon, Exalted One, whispered another. A burst of white energy poured through the host, captivated by the Energizer's jubilant vision of an exploding planet, flooding oceans, and shaking ground—as the overused and overmodified support systems of the small planet unraveled. Terrors visualized by ancient, bewildered prophets would come to pass: atmosphere, oceans and terra firma would be obliterated in cataclysmic bursts of physical and chemical disruption.

Just doing Our job, the Energizer agreed. After all, it had charge of this miserable chunk of matter. Humankind had been given mastery of this little orb for a short time and humankind would be its end. The Energizer and its hosts merely helped the Keeper complete a project S/HE had predicted eons ago.

Remember, Yessers, all will be Ours, unembodied and Ours forever, the Energizer sang. *We simply hasten their foolish destructions. Only incompetence has thwarted progress thus far.*

Do not fail or the Abyss will consume you, It warned its relieved flunkies as it moved through the spirit realm towards a happier event—a pep rally with the carefully selected spirits who inspired and motivated delegates to the upcoming TRI-WAC.

chapter Sixteen
DELEGATION

*E**very tongue and nation, indeed.* Energizer chuckled as it enfolded princes and powers in a rush of energy, the gathering node filling with hot waves of superiority and satisfaction.

These emotions poured into the delegates gathered for the daily Pre-WAC preconference briefing. What a rush! Hundreds of the world's greatest thinkers joined virtually via technology. HEADs buzzed as the delegates reviewed the slated protocols.

"I move consideration of Directive XX.iii – the Wilds Development Protocol," said Heddy LaMar, who represented Babel II's Taming the Wilds (TW) faction. "We need unanimous agreement—any dissent will incite the Nature Heads."

"You're having a little trouble managing Greenies in your Babel, Delegate LaMar," sneered Kazimir Pasternak, Babel I 2.1 delegate. "What's this we hear of an illegal Wilds visit? How can your citizens flagrantly violate worldwide agreements?"

"I suggest that Babel II security follow Babel I 1.1," said Wang Hu, another TW member. "We have detained all Wild supporters until the TRI-WAC is completed."

"We cannot allow threats to this wonderful and untapped economic resource," added Hu.

"Threats to *your* economic resource, Delegate," sneered Delegate Horoto Suzuki. "Mountain-top cabinettes on the Zhangjiajie Wild pillars— 'own your own piece of paradise,'" he said, quoting Wu's promo viz.

Hu sputtered. "Prosperity benefits all," he said. "Not all understand this."

"So Babel I violates the Code of Civilian Rights to control public ignorance?" snapped Delegate Fatma Sahin. "Sounds like police state propaganda to me."

The harmonious atmosphere dissolved into bitter reflections, buzzing side conversations, accusations and doubts as old animosities stirred the virtual assembly.

Within these human energies, the Energizer's forces nearly drowned in tidal waves of animosity and confusion. The human tendency to strife and chaos could be useful. But not today. The Energizer itself pulled away from the rabble, and collected itself. It signaled a key Influencer, drawing it away from the flood.

Time to intervene.

The Influencer sent calming thoughts to its host, Dong Jun, Babel I lead representative and Vice Moderator for the upcoming TRI-WAC. He spoke up.

"Yes, Wild supporters in Babel I 1.1 have been detained," Dong said. "But only for their protection. I agree with Babel II Delegate LaMar.

Wilds are a source of dissent. Once we assimilate them, we move on to something we all agree on: progress and prosperity for all!"

Words from the older statesman, founder of the TRI-WACs, had a calming influence.

"We have worldwide cooperation," Dong continued. "High Counselors of Security in every Babel are monitoring distractions. Curfews have been established prior to convention departure. There will be no more focus on Wilds outside the permitted demonstrations."

Dong adjusted his HEAD and dignitaries worldwide gazed at his serene face. "I would hear a motion to move the Wilds Development Protocol for preapproval by the TRI-WAC," he said.

"So moved!" "Second!" Several delegates spoke at once.

As he led the assembly through voting protocols, Dong expected (and received) a unanimous vote. He felt slight contempt for his colleagues. So childish, so emotional—but so desperate to rise above their squalid, squabbling past. Move forward, and they'd all fall quickly into line.

Dong knew how to push the levers and move urbanity forward. When the TRI-WAC convened Sunday, all dissent would be settled. Questions and concerns that were raised were only part of the show. Worldwide democracy in action.

Well done, said the Energizer, sending a wave of euphoria through the gathered Powers that passed on to the delegates as renewed pride and satisfaction. Progress would continue.

Keren and her companions returned to class, shaken by the encounter with Counselor Dred. Two Security Yessers had slipped into each Period V class. Keren found the new Phys Ed Aids particularly ridiculous.

Snark had told them a citywide curfew would be imposed until delegate departure from Babel II at 0800 Saturday. Only preapproved demonstrations would be allowed.

At precisely 1600 hours, wrist tabs began flashing.

SECURITY LEVEL VI IS IN EFFECT CITY-WIDE UNTIL 0800 SATURDAY. TAKE AUTO DIRECTLY TO RESIDENCE AND REMAIN UNTIL MORNING COMMUTE TIME.

Keren sighed and rolled her eyes at Caleb. No walking home today. How will we get to the Wilds? she wondered. Sensors and drones would observe flying dinosaurs. How could they leave without detection?

Caleb read her thoughts. "No worries," he said. "The Keeper never does the same thing twice. There will be a way for us to go. Go home, do homework, hang out with the family and get ready. We will be called."

"Called?" Keren asked.

"The Keeper's messengers transcend time and space," he said.

"You mean like that old read, *A Wrinkle in Time?*" Keren asked.

"L'Engle envisioned something; no one really knows what it is," Caleb said. "Old writings speak to it. Ancient Celtics referred to 'thin places' where other dimensions connect to our own. Perhaps we each get a 'thin place.'"

Keren remembered another phrase. "I am the *door* of the sheep," she said. "Maybe a door. But geez, Caleb, I like animals, but do we have to be sheep?"

"I felt like a 'lamb led to slaughter' facing Counselor Dred," Caleb said as they slipped onto the Auto and tapped the nav pad for their stops. The programming permitted group travel on a shared ribbon— called "grouping"—although sudden ribbon splits at the parting always provided a shock. (Couples learned *not* to hold hands when traveling towards different destinations!)

"What did you start to say when he asked if you went to the Desert Wild, Cal?"

"I didn't have a creative answer," Caleb admitted. "I thought I'd tell him 'I'm not a morning person and would not be up at 0600' but that sounded zomboid."

"So we do our usual stuff at home and just wait?"

"That's the plan," Caleb said. "Take a warming wrap for your journey," he added. "But I think the Keeper will supply what we need. We must supply the courage."

chapter Seventeen
NIGHT MOVES

T he evening dragged on. The students had an OA Math exam for Friday morning, but found it hard to study.

Caleb lounged in his ergo-chair, picking at a practice problem, when the equation melted into Irving Fidget's earnest face. "Lo, Cal, welcome to a team meeting," the geek said. Immediately the OA Bio class appeared around him.

"Whoa!" said Caleb.

"Cynthia and I found this new channel," said Irving. "Not sure how. But I thought we should check in."

"You sure Intercept isn't monitoring us?" asked Timmie, brow creased in concern.

"This frequency doesn't exist in the world," said Cynthia. "It transcends any spyware the Dominion has."

"Projection is on track," she added. "We've located every delegate's HEAD and the top Yessers in each of the Babels. We accelerated their receptors, and retuned for the Sunday Wild broadcast."

"Projection intercept on freeze status until then," Irving added. "No need to stir up the Dominion with strange signals."

"Irv, could you patch us into your new channel for a couple of kiloseconds?" asked Marc, the Sim Team leader. "We have some fine-tuning to do on the Wilds experience—adding sounds and sensory stims. We lost most of today to Yesser distractions and then couldn't get past the intercept this afternoon."

"We specialize in unconventional channels." Cynthia gave her trademark geek grin, a reminder that she and Irving worked in tandem.

Yessers are no match for the dynamic duo, Caleb thought.

"The rescue team is on track to leave at 2300," Caleb said. "I have no idea where we're going. I hope you can find us in the Citadel."

"Gotcha covered," Irving said. "We hacked Citadel security before the Yessers started jamming channels. We've had to patch in from our new freq, but it's easy. Even you right-brainers will do fine. In fact..." He fumbled at his desk and then held up a tiny earpiece. "Remember these durky earsets that came with the wrist tabs?" he asked. "Find yours, wherever you stashed them—and wear them. We will be a guiding voice in your pointed ears."

"Just like the Prophetess, but less attractive," Sal said.

"Slick. The OA Rescue Team with matching earrings," Arana said. "Should I accessorize with matching tights and wall shoes? Caleb will look so cute on the security viz—"

"I have a gut feeling the Yessers won't see us," Caleb replied. "I hope I'm right."

"Will you keep us in the loop, Irving?" Keren asked.

"Sorry, you guys are on your own," Irving said. "We can't tune in to more than one place. You and Bopha are going worldwide."

"Don't worry, Keren," Caleb said. "Your Assistance will be in several places at once, anywhere S/HE is needed."

"Here's our itinerary." Bopha's neat table showed on the virtch screen. "We've picked Wilds within travel distance of a Babel municipality. We found Babel VII is just a few kilometers from Antarctic Wild—swimming distance for the penguins and sea lions. I hope we find a few left."

"And Babel V 1.7 – right in the heart of Amazonia Wild – has grown to five million!" said Keren. "Most live under the central dome. Paradise thrives around them, but they never see it."

"They will when the Wildlings come calling," said Bopha.

"Did you hear that we are all going to the TRI-WAC with Dr. Dierk?" ask Caleb.

"I didn't hear that exactly," Lizzie said. "I heard 'be ready to gather' on Saturday. No specifics."

An impatient voice called outside Caleb's portal: "Caleb, dinner time!"

"Gotta go, brainies," he said. "Let's meet again soon."

"Count on it," said Irving.

"May the Keeper preserve us," Sal said, her voice quavering. Sal, a champion sprinter, could outrun anyone. But as she envisioned fleeing through a maze of dark passageways pursued by armed Yessers and unknown terrors, her heart dropped.

Caleb felt her apprehension. "Don't worry, wild ones, it won't be any worse than viz games," he said. "Once you meet the Keeper, fear will vanish. Embrace the adventure." He clicked off his tab and his classmates disappeared.

Outside his door, Nora tapped a toe. "Is math that enticing?" she asked. "You've delayed dinner, and made me late."

"Another date, Sis?" Nora's pretty face flushed. He knew she preferred her boyfriend to school stuff. Enduring her final year at HERC 1100, Nora wanted it over.

"Just the B-ball game—if Management doesn't waste our time with a civics lecture," said Nora.

"They want us informed on the TRI-WAC," Caleb said. "It will change our lives in a lot of ways."

"I really doubt that stuffy delegates passing protocols, and gas, will have one iota of influence on *my* life," said Nora. "I about died of boredom at the assembly this morning. Death by droning dignitary." She mimed hanging herself.

"Really?" her brother asked. "Ours intrigued everyone; quite the wonder woman."

"Oh yeah, you got Dr. Perkins, didn't you? MERCs got the glamour queen! She does look more like a sim star than a policy drone," Nora said. "Gorgeous face and toned gym bod all wrapped up in a power suit. She actually said something interesting? What in Babel could that be?"

Not a good idea to evoke Nora's interest, Caleb thought. Nora had a quick mind, when not distracted by friends and social dramas.

"She assigned us each a secret mission for the TRI-WAC," said Caleb, pulling an imaginary hat over his eyes and touching a finger to his lips.

"Why don't you start your mission right now—on another planet," said Nora.

Dad tapped the table. "Okay kids, let's offer thanks."

Nora raised her eyebrows only slightly as they all clasped hands, and recited "Great and Good." The Bensons kept the old traditions.

Caleb stretched out on the sleeping mat. He wanted to bag a little sleep. Nora would return after he left, but he doubted she would do a bed check. Dad, who had early morning rounds at the central medical complex, had already gone to bed. Mom, the night owl, worked on her manuscript about Urban Depressive Syndrome. If she kept her usual routine, Caleb could leave and return before she turned in.

He wore a breathable body suit he used for afternoon park runs. He had programmed his wrist tab and put in the ear bud. He slipped a cooled water bag onto his belt band. Not quite the heavily armed hero in a sci-fi vid, he thought. But, ready.

Caleb.

He sat up and saw a radiant figure hovering by his mat. The fierce face shone too brightly for Caleb to make out its features. "I am the Guide," the figure said.

Caleb nodded, and got to his feet. "Come," the vision said.

Caleb felt himself moving with tremendous speed. The Guide ushered him through a corridor of blinding light; the colors flashed by in nauseating patterns. He closed his eyes as they hurtled along. The great rush slowed to a stop. In the fading light, he saw Arana and Sal. "Hey team," he whispered. They stood together, shadowy figures, not quite materialized.

"Cal, where in heck are we?" asked Sal.

"I think we are on our way," Arana said as they hurtled forward.

Is this how the Keeper's messengers travel? Cal wondered as they flew along.

Abruptly, they stood in a dark hallway, most likely deep within the Citadel. They sensed, but could not see, the presence of their Guide. "I expect Irv and Cyn will be tuning in to us," Caleb whispered. "They targeted the area where Dr. Dierk is being held."

"Why couldn't the Guides just stage this rescue themselves? Why do they need us?" Sal whispered as Cal fiddled with his tab.

"The Keeper likes to work through people. S/HE rarely does anything without human cooperation. Maybe because S/HE gave us responsibility for the planet."

"Probably why most things on the planet are so messed up," Arana said. "*Not* much human cooperation."

As they huddled against a wall, their tabs suddenly glowed yellow, and a virtual map of the massive Citadel site hung in the air before them. A "You are Here" label showed their location. "Nice touch, Irv," Cal said.

Their Guide had deposited them near a storage area in Level V of the massive security complex. Their schematic showed a High Security Detention Area—Dr. Dierk's likely location—right below them in Level VI.

"So just how do we—" Cal started to ask and shut up, hearing voices coming their way.

"Run for it!" Arana whispered.

No. Their Guide's voiceless command. *Stand and watch.* They froze, blinking in the glare, as bright lights switched on and a troupe of Worker Yessers walked towards them.

Caleb looked into empty eyes, realizing the supply crew could not see them. They continued past the students, discussing "TRI-WAC arsenal restock."

"Are we ghosts?" Sal whispered, after the crew voices faded down the hall.

You are Guided and where We are, you are also, the Guide answered.

Not much of an answer, Caleb thought. Maybe the Guide saw no need to explain the inexplicable. Perhaps they remained in that different dimension where the Guides traveled. It felt safer.

"I think we are still alive," Caleb answered, "but we have protected status."

"Hey troops, stop with the yapping. Ready to find Dr. Dierk?" Irving's voice interjected. Again the Citadel schematic appeared before them.

"Looks like there's a crawl space between the levels for maintenance and repairs," Arana noted. "Am I the designated crawler?"

"Yup. The entrance is right behind you," Irving said. "That's why the Guide landed you here. You can only enter Level VI on the EL with a security clearance or you set off alarms. Arana, slide down to Level VI. We will help you disengage the security system; then Cal and Sal can take the ped route to Level VI."

"Ped route?" Sal asked.

"Around the next corner. Emergency stairs between levels," said Cynthia. "You can use them once alarms are deactivated. I have shut down everything I can from remote and you aren't showing on their monitors, but there's a manual override for Level VI. Someone has to flip that."

"Too bad you don't have an earring for Dr. Dierk—you could just tell him to put out the welcome mat," Sal said.

"Well, there goes our 'flipper,'" Sal added as Arana found the dimly lit hatch and yanked open the cover. A vertical vent descended rapidly.

"Flipper's a dolphin, I'm a spider," Arana corrected. "Whooeee!" She produced a climber's cord from her belt. "No probbo. Slick descendo!" She attached a small pulley to the industrial-grade handle on the portal, allowing her to check the speed of her headfirst descent into the dark tunnel below. "Don't worry. These techniques have been perfected by multiple UrbEx adventurers." She dived into the tunnel.

The Yessers probably used a propulsion–restraint system for more measured movement through the vertical tunnel, but Arana loved the thrill of flying face down, checking her speed at intervals with little tugs on her pull cord. She jerked her way down the tunnel, bumping and bouncing off the sides. At the next level, the tunnel tilted upwards towards the Level VI portal. Arana pulled her cord taut and crouched in front of the portal. At her push, it opened outwards into another hallway.

"I'm in the hall, Irving," she whispered as she stepped out into pitch darkness.

"Drop!" she heard Cynthia's sharp whisper. She flattened against the floor as a search ray buzzed above her head.

"Stay down, and watch your tab," the geek ordered. A new map lit up in front of her. She crouched before a circular foyer, ringed by a dozen doors. Each led to a suite of rooms, occupied by a detainee.

"Irv is briefing the team on your escape, once you get the doc," said Cynthia. "I'm your security support for this."

"Hey Cyn, why don't I just free all the prisoners?" Arana said.

"No!" said Cynthia. "Not everyone here is a political prisoner. There are some dangerous characters.

"See the red console on your map?" Cynthia continued. "Can you locate it in the room? It should be right by the EL entrance." Arana saw a faint red glow on the map directly across from the vent.

"Let me give you some focused light," Cynthia said, and Arana's wrist tab emitted a small beam. She directed it across the circular room and made out the arches of the EL entrance. Her light outlined a panel of instruments. Using the beam as a guide, Arana worm-crawled towards the panel, buzzing search beams crisscrossing the space above her.

"How do I touch this thing without getting buzzed?" Arana asked once she got to the panel.

"I'm locked into your tab remote," Cynthia said. "I've got manual override programmed in. Point your tab at the panel when I tell you."

Arana wondered how Cynthia had figured out configuration details for the highest security building in the entire Dominion government complex. Cynthia apparently read her mind. "The Yessers document everything. You just have to be good online, and have a little expertise at hacking."

Cynthia seemed buzzed that her friends' lives depended on her skills. Arana heard her friend humming happily as she worked her tab. "Got it," Cynthia said. "See that little light on your tab?" A blue light glowed on Arana's wrist. "Aim it towards the panel, and it will locate the override."

Arana followed her instructions and the blue light lit up a single button on the console. With a short BZZZZT! the beams above her vanished.

"Security down!" she said. She stood up.

"Great job, Arana; stand by," Cynthia told her. "Rescue team enroute."

Caleb and Sal crept down steep stairs, resisting the impulse to bound. "These are fun!" Caleb whispered. "I wish we had them in the MERC!"

"They knew you guys would bounce up and down the stairs all day," Sal said. "Security risk—injured kids from stair falls. Treds are so much safer, and *so much* more boring."

"Better keep it quiet," Caleb reflected. "The monitors must be super-sensitive in here—"

"The monitors are down, but only for five more hectoseconds," Irving's voice vibrated in his ear.

"Welcome to Detention," Arana greeted her team. "We have a Monty Hall Problem," she said, recalling an OA Math exercise. "Which door do we choose?"

Every door looked alike.

"Let me help you," whispered Irving. "I've programmed in Dr. Dierk's brainwave patterns from simulator test runs. Sal, turn your tab towards each door, and hold for a dekasecond."

Sal did as directed. Her tab glowed, projecting a faint beam. A dim red light flashed on her tab as she scanned each door. Each time, Irving said, "Nope."

After 7 dekaseconds of eternity, Sal saw a green flash on her tab for a door. "Good job, Irv," she said. "Green is go."

Cal tapped the entrance panel. The door slid open.

They stood in a small foyer. Moving inside, they saw a figure on the sleeping platform.

"Dr. Dierk! Wake up!" Caleb stage whispered.

Their teacher bolted up. "What in wild acres?" he sputtered. "Caleb?"

"Shhh, Doc," Caleb whispered. "You called me, remember? We came for you."

"Wow. You really did." The teacher, now fully awake, got to his feet, pulled on his day suit and then gathered his rescuers in a bear hug.

"You really did," Dr. Dierk repeated.

"I see you harnessed Arana's exploratory energies for the cause," Dr. Dierk quipped as he flipped his Wilds files from the desk comp onto his wrist tab.

"You should have seen her flying down that access vent," Sal said.

"Will your Guide be able to spirit us all away?" Dierk asked as they hurried up the stairs to Level V. As they got to the top, Irv announced they had two hectoseconds before bio-monitoring resumed. A zero-read from Dierk's quarters would trigger alarms, and seal off the detention area.

"The Guide disappeared when we went downstairs," Caleb said, not the least breathless as they topped the stairs to Level V. "Irv mapped our course to the access portal, but we're going to be running through security forces when the alarms sound."

On Level V, Irv directed them to an EL door. "This is an unmarked security EL. It's the only direct way in or out," he said. "You summon it From Level II, where the Security Yessers live."

"Why is it here?" Sal asked as the doors opened and they stepped into the vertical cube.

"I brought it for you," Cynthia chimed in. "I tapped into the EL system. When the detention alarm goes off—in two dekaseconds now—this EL will take you right up."

chapter Seventeen
WORLD WILDLING TOUR

Mother smiled, proud of the fresh greens she brought to the table. "These are all from our own garden plot," she said.

"Want soldier food!" Tug screamed. "Want MREs! Not sissy grasses!"

"Oh Tug, no one eats MREs now," Mother said. "You're playing too many old Soldier Sims. Big soldiers eat their greens!"

"You are a good soldier, Tug," Keren said, hoping to placate the noisy tot.

"Tug secret agent soldier with Spy Keh-wan!" Tug grinned.

Oh no, what did I start? "Tug, did you dream about being spies with me? I bet you had a big dream!"

"Not dream—Tug and Keh-wan spy last night!" Tug insisted. "Tug patrol house, and Keh-wan take secret message." He tried to imitate his big sister's voice. "Tug, you stealth patrol on tiger paws." He jumped down and toddled around the table on his "paws."

Dad burst out laughing. "First a Wildling biologist, and now a tiger in the family. Tigers like meat best, Tug, but sometimes they eat grass. Grasses are medicine for their tummies. Come back to the table. Daddy will play tiger with you after dinner. Okay?"

"Play tiger wi' Da!" Tug crawled back onto his ergo seat, which raised him to table level. He took a bite of salad, grimaced, but swallowed the "tiger medicine." "Want meat, want meat."

"Tigers eat deer and boar, Tug," Keren noted. "Eat your boar-burger."

She passed a platter of soy burgers and her brother grabbed one. "Boh bugger, rowwr!" He took a big bite, chewing with his teeth showing in a grimace.

"If the Wilds Protocol passes the TRI-WAC, the tiger habitat will vanish," said Keren. "We'll only see tigers in Zo-Parks."

"By the way, the Urban Arts Society will participate in the Save Our Wilds Demo Saturday," Dad said. "Do you want to go with us?"

"Uh, yes," Keren said. She didn't know how Saturday would roll out, but sometime that weekend she expected to be on the other side of the planet.

"Do you really think it will change anything?" she asked. "Don't the WACs enact everything proposed? We have freedom of expression, but no freedom of change. The Dominion does what they want. And they want to destroy the Wilds!"

"The Pro-urbans dominate," Mother agreed. "But it's just a movement. And a movement can have a change of direction—or a change of heart."

"If Babelites understood this trashing of support systems built into this planet—maybe they'd change," Keren said. "But most think our techno-fixes make life better. Never mind all the 'system down' times."

"Ah yes, the myths of progress and control." Dad sighed. "They played well with the Egyptians, the Romans, and with every previous civilization. Now we've bought into it worldwide."

"I don't think we all bought in, Jim," Mother said. "It's those who profit directly in the short run. We must show the long-term costs."

"Mother you're just like the Science Heads of the last century," Keren said. "They warned about impacts on atmospheric and climatic balance; they tried to educate. No one listened.

"Now every Babel has a climate control generating station to offset the violent storms, winds and hurricanes from the disruptions our ancestors unleashed using so much fossil fuel," Keren added. "That's why the urban-ites want to move underground. We've unleashed the negative forces of nature, so now we are trying to separate ourselves from our mistakes."

"Well, thank Creation the depletion of the petro sources forced the shift to renewables," Dad said. "Atmospheric scientists say the balance has improved."

"That's the problem, Dad, the earth and its systems are so giving and so forgiving," Keren said. "We create a disaster, a whole civilization crashes, something recalibrates, and we forget all about the damage."

Tug changed the subject. "Tiger eat boh bugga and deah bugga, Da! Can Tiger hunt for more deah?" He jumped down from his ergo-chair and resumed creeping on his tiger paws. "Rowwwr, rowwwr," he growled.

"Tiger Tug, find a hiding place and Daddy deer will come by soon," Dad said, grinning as the toddler dropped to hands and knees and slunk out of the room, growling softly.

Keren finished her salad and a little burger. "Could I be excused? I have homework." Mother nodded. Keren grabbed the empty plates, put them on the wash-belt, and bounded up the stairs to her room. No EL-lifts in the Anderson home.

"Creeping tigers and bounding deer!" Mother said. "We have our own Wildlings!"

"We haven't destroyed their habitat here," Dad said, moving leftovers to containers and setting the table wiper before he dropped to his hands and knees and crawled out to meet Tiger Tug, waiting in ambush. "Baaa," Keren heard his loud falsetto. "Baaa, baaa."

"I thought you were a deer," she called down.

"I don't know what deer sound like," Dad called back. "Baaa, baaaaaaah."

"Eeeeehhhhhhhhhhuuhhhhhh," Keren corrected. "Deer sort of squeak."

"Behhhhhhh, behhhhhh," Dad tried, eliciting a high-pitched "Rowwwr!" from Tug. A thud, sounds of a tussle, Dad's laughter.

Then *click-click-click* as Mother's ergo chair moved over to her desk for the evening accounting.

Keren hurtled through singing space, ushered by the Guide. She glimpsed Bopha's shadowy outline against the color collage flashing by. The blur faded, sickening motion slowed and Bopha's figured solidified beside her own. They emerged into daylight, blinking like riders abruptly deposited aboveground from a subterranean Tred. Sun rays streamed through the canopy, highlighting a few waxy leaves of small plants. Moist air like a hot towel smacked Keren's face. Rubbing her eyes, she glanced around a small clearing surrounded by buttressed, tent-like roots at eye level. Craning her head, she gazed up at towering Dipterocarp trees, giant monarchs of the tropical forests. Keren pulled out her cap and fanned her face. She noticed Bopha unfolded and donned her wide brimmed field hat. "Whew!" Bopha said.

Sudden chattering, then a sound like a trumpet blast. An elephant thundered into the clearing, a trio of primates clinging to her back: an orangutan, a gibbon and a red leaf monkey. The elephant bowed, her passengers slid down and stood before the girls. "Welcome, friends of the Keeper," they said.

"I never conversed with a gibbon before!" Bopha said. She gave a courtesy bow, hands in prayer posture.

"Greetings, friends," Keren said. "The Keeper enlists your help to save this Wild."

"We lead in the Tropical Wild," Red Monkey said. "What is the threat, and how can we help?"

Gibbon took the young women's hands, and led them to a log in the shade. "Sit, enjoy our refreshments, and tell us of the Keeper's plan."

A cadre of macaques entered the clearing with fresh mangos and coconut shells filled with milk.

"The Keeper thinks we humans are too removed from the Wilds," Bopha said. "We live in protected Babels. We no longer breathe clean air or see Wildlings, except in Zo-Parks. We live in fear of the Keeper's gifts."

"Now our kind plans to destroy your habitat," Keren added. "They want to build Babels into the Wilds."

Gibbon's face wrinkled further. "What can we do?" she asked.

"You can help us bring the Wilds back to the people," Bopha said.

Discussion followed on logistical details. Who would go and how to traverse the great distance between Tropical Wild and the Babel I municipalities.

No problem for the cuckoos, barbets, hornbills, swifts, shrikes, darters, whistlers, magpies, mynas, flycatchers and other birds.

"Some of our migrants travel thousands of your kilometers on their regular world tour," Red Monkey observed. "A short flight to a Babel is no problem for the bird brigade; they routinely pass through the cities. But our land travelers are limited."

"The tigers will lead," Orangutan said. "They can swim the rivers and streams for more than 15 kilometers and then travel on land to the Babel. The elephants can also travel far. But we should also send the sun bears, who move slowly. Friend marten, mongoose and fox are very quick but too small to travel long distance."

"And what about our forest travelers?" asked Gibbon, brow more furrowed. "The paradise tree snake can lead the reptiles, flying between the trees followed by the gliding lizards and geckos. Many of us can also swing through the trees with our cousins, the lemurs, orangutans and macaques. But so much land is cleared near the closest Babel, how will they cross there?"

"The Keeper said gather at the Wild boundary by 1200 hours Saturday and S/HE will provide a way," Keren said. "A Guide brought us here by a different way from earth or sky. Another time a prehistoric flying lizard carried us home. I do not know how you will get to the Babel but if you are willing, you will get there."

Red Monkey laughed. "No one knows what the Keeper does next. We will obey the Keeper and come to the border of our Wild on Saturday."

"We must assemble our friends from across the Wild," Gibbon said. "It will take time. I begin the summons now."

Leaving the visitors, she leaped to a tree and quickly scrambled up the red trunk.

WhhooooWhoooWhooop! WhoooWhoooWhooop! WhoooWhoooWhooop! WhoooWhoooWhoooWhoop! Her whistling call soared, echoing through the forest.

As the forest resounded with answering whoops and whirrs, the Keeper's summons made its way across the Tropical Wild.

Red Monkey and Orangutan offered a low bow as Keren and Bopha departed, gathered up by their Guide and projected into the corridor of colors.

"I enjoyed the Tropical Wild, I can handle the Wet Tropic Wild, and I'm excited to see the Floating Islands Wild," Bopha said as they sped along through the corridor of lights. "But I am not looking forward to the Antarctic Wild!"

"That's why the Keeper picked us to work together," Keren said. "I get dizzy in the heat but I like the cold. Caleb said the Guide will keep us warm."

"I brought my therms just in case," Bopha said.

Antarctic, Polar and Sub-Arctic Wilds felt chilly. Fortunately, the therms, warming cloak and face coverings seemed enhanced, and nobody froze.

"What blows my mind," whispered Bopha, "is polar bears conversing with seals—instead of eating them."

"They both have an interest in keeping ice floes," Keren said. "And they can certainly keep them." She appreciated the Guide's firm grip holding them steady on an icy island two meters square.

"When the Keeper is around, Wildlings lose interest in eating each other," Keren said. "I will always remember dancing with coyotes and rabbits in Desert Wild."

In this supernatural time, even insects cooperated. At one meeting held in predawn darkness, clouds of sparkling fireflies lit the gloom.

Bopha, veteran of tropical explorations, expressed shock at leeches standing on their tails to listen. "I can't believe they are staying on the ground," she told Keren. "Usually they come swinging, end-to-end, right up your leg. Everyone is minding their manners."

"Even the army ants," Keren agreed. The fierce red creatures lined up in rows, listening but making no hostile moves towards human or Wildling.

"I hope they send a platoon into Babel I 1.1," Bopha said. "They would be a real show stopper."

Every Wilds visit turned out to be a biologist's dream. In the Tasmanian Wild, they met the famous Tasmanian Devil, accompanied by a tiger, an eastern quol, a wombat and a pademelon. When Keren properly named the pouched creature, the pademelon gave a hop of exuberance and a thump of her great tail. "You would not *believe* how many tourists call us 'kangaroos,'" she complained.

At the Floating Island Wild, they met atop a 1000-meter tall quartz sandstone pillar overlooking the great reserve. "How did you guys get here?" Keren asked the Wildling collection: a pig-tailed macaque, a slow-tailed Loris and a clouded leopard representing the predator division. "Same way you did," purred the leopard. "When the Keeper summons, the way is provided."

He assured Keren the Wildlings could muster a large delegation to the TRI-WAC. "We've never been invited before," he added. "We'll spread the word."

The shifting time zones spun Karen's brain. "Suspend disbelief," Bopha urged her; she consulted her spinning timepiece, shaking her head, as their Guide moved them. They might have selected the Wilds to visit, but the Guide moved them in an unknowable pattern. According to Keren's tab and the sun position, the first Wilds visit happened noon Friday and others the night before.

"The Keeper uses time as needed," Bopha reminded her as they arrived in a dark rainforest shortly after visiting the chilly but sunny Polar Wild.

"S/HE doesn't seem to obey physics," Keren said. "But maybe linear motion is just one of our simplistic human ideas."

"You think time is linear, too," Bopha said. "But in every Wild, we have had plenty of time to visit the Wildlings, discuss plans, enjoy refreshments and take a little tour."

"There is no way we have visited all these places," Keren said, consulting her timepiece again. "My head hurts!"

"Don't overthink it," Bopha advised. "Westerners are too linear. Accept the gift. Right now we are living outside of our human limits. We would never visit all these places in our lifetime. Enjoy the moment."

They landed on a stark mountain, and Bopha gaped at the Welcome Team.

"WOW!" Bopha enthused as two rattlesnakes slithered towards them, then rose up on their tails. "Greetingssssss, emissssssssaries of the Keeper!" they hissed together, emphasizing the words with their rattles while bowing heads in sinuous unison.

To Keren's delight, Coati stood behind the snakes, grinning and waving his tail. The Desert delegation included a javelina, a mule deer, a coyote, a horned toad and a scorpion. They met on the mount where Keren and Caleb saw the Keeper just that morning. The Guide had saved the best for last.

"Welcome back," Coati said to Keren. "No dance tonight. Maybe Sunday!"

"We are honored to visit your city," the rattlers hissed. "The Wilds are close, but your kind live in an artificial world. We will bring reality."

Bopha considered the prospect of rattlers, cougars and coyotes startling their fellow Babel denizens. "It would be nice if the centipedes, scorpions and tarantulas could come too, but they don't move very fast—"

"The deer will transport a few crawlers for the full desert effect," Coati promised, and the scorpion waved her arched tail in agreement.

"You already knew these, uh...folks?" Bopha asked as the Guide whisked them off.

"These are the ones we danced with, here in the Desert Wild just— wow, just yesterday morning," Keren replied. "It's like I have known Coati all my life."

Bopha nodded as they flew in the Guide's wake. "To feast together is to be family," Bopha said. "Although..." A little grin lit up Bopha's round face. "...not sure I want to observe the rattlers feasting."

"You're not like Duane—no feeding mice to your pet snakes," Keren said.

"The Humane Pets Directive banned live feeding," Bopha said. "There's a plant protein robo-mouse. It squeaks like prey but it's not alive. So nothing suffers when it is swallowed."

"That's ironic," Keren said. "Creating artificial prey for pets in our artificial world."

She saw Bopha's slender form fading away from her. "Your night's mission is complete, daughters of the Keeper," the Guide said. "Stay alert."

Without a chance for goodbye or hand smack, Keren found herself home. She looked at the glowing time in her darkened room: approximately 2257. Wow. She had arrived at home approximately two hectoseconds before she had begun her tour.

Downstairs she heard the hiss of the tread; Mother started her Simwalk. The quiet upstairs indicated that Tug and Dad slept.

Peeking out of her travel pouch: a desert poppy and a few tan and black hairs from Coati's tail.

chapter nineteen
FOREVER FRIDAY

The warship headed straight for Caleb. A hard shove, and he skimmed along under the craft.

"Drop and roll!" screamed Arana and they hit the walkway under the portal, rolling under the cruiser into space. They freefell, hurtling past the Citadel towards the city below.

The force that threw them out of danger now enfolded them, slowing their descent, until they hovered just above street level.

BZZZZZZZZMMMMMMMM! Caleb craned his head to see white flashes around Counselor Dred's aircraft, now hundreds of meters above them.

Time to go, children, the Guide said. *Well done.*

"Later, team," Caleb said, smiling at the others.

For a moment, they hung in the sky above the city, and then four fugitives dispersed, heading four separate ways.

Back in his room, Caleb tabbed Marc, Sim Team lead.

"Cheese, Cal, it's 0130 hours. Kinda bad time for a social call." Marc appeared, yawning loudly.

"We got Dr. Dierk!" Caleb said, grinning and pumping his right fist up. "We have new data for the Sim. Dierk assimilated them with all his free time. I'm sending them. Stand by."

"Where is Dierk?" Marc asked as his tab lit up with the data-send.

"Desert Wild," Caleb said. "I don't think it's safe for him to go home yet."

"I wanta hear your debrief," Marc said. "Much later this morning—after Math."

Caleb stretched out on his sleeping platform. Two wild nights, back to back. How would he get through another school day?

Friday dragged.

Keren and Caleb rode the Auto to MERC 1102. No walking allowed.

"Nothing to see anyway," Keren said, grieving the demise of their favorite pocket park. But she enjoyed the tale of Caleb's successful mission.

"So Dr. Dierk is in Desert Wild?" she asked. "We went there last. I must have missed him by a few kiloseconds!"

"Amazing how the Keeper works this time stuff," Caleb admitted. "For the Citadel, we left at 2300 Thursday and got back around 0130 this morning. About 10 kiloseconds actual time, which makes sense. But you and Bopha got back *before* you left."

"We must have visited one hundred Wilds last night," Keren said. "We had time with all the Wildlings. It's like a wonderful dream. But I'm ironed flat."

"I'm dreading today," Caleb said.

They filed into OA Biology class. Everyone wanted an update, but no one said a word.

Mincer, acting with her usual clueless self-confidence, administered a "pop quiz" on asexual reproduction. As if anyone cared. They jumped right to it, raising hands and shouting out answers, acting like trained seals barking for fish. Mincer beamed with smug satisfaction at the "class participation."

The OA Math exam turned out worse than Keren anticipated with story problems to decipher, solve and justify from the long list of postulates and theorems they had memorized. Why not just solve the stupid problem? Keren thought. How could anyone concentrate on this silliness with the future of Wilds at stake?

In Current Events, Mr. Prig switched on Newsflash for the latest TRI-WAC preparations.

"URP authorities have expanded the Accelerated Urban Improvement Project," Eddie Anchor reported, standing before a wasteland of toppled trees and flattened ground. "Look at those excavators! They've restructured 13 pocket parks just this morning!

"In other developments, John Snitch has just been promoted to Head Ranger of Desert Wild. With his background in Park Engineering,

Mr. Snitch will oversee transition after the Wild Development Protocol is formalized this week. Mr. Snitch?"

"Thanks Eddie—yes. We're ready to give Babel II the urban playground the city needs," said the Yesser, posing in front of a grader. "We realize the closest Wild to Babel II has been 'locked up' far too long. Only hikers and Nature Heads currently use it."

Keren's gloom changed to delight at the last clip: bright laser flares outside the Citadel. "At 0115 this morning, Newsflash captured buzzing lasers in the heart of the city," said reporter Noreen Nose. "Dominion Security launched an Orange Alert practice invasion and a simulated power outage."

Counselor Dred appeared on the cam, blowing a smokescreen about public safety and civic defense from his hovercraft in front of the Citadel.

Keren wondered if Dred believed his own stories. Hard to read his smug smile. He must think his blasters got Dr. Dierk.

She longed for Nutri-Break, when they could regroup. From the frazzed out expressions around the classroom, most of the kids didn't realize Dierk had escaped.

Caleb's subtle thumbs up reassured those who did not yet know the whole story.

"That liar!" Keren got to say when they had gathered in the break room.

"Now we see how the Dominion operates," Paul Wonk said. "Ninety percent of what they tell us is PR fantasy talk."

"The truth is *so much* more interesting," Sal agreed. She recounted their flight through flashing corridors, arrival in the Citadel, Yessers marching right past them and Arana disappearing into the dark shaft.

Arana, more doer than teller, let her friend gab on.

"Poor Dr. Dierk, we gave him a fright," Sal continued. "Then we hustled him out. Only one EL out of the place—but Cyn hacked it. When the alarms went off, the EL took us right up."

"Did you have to fight Security Yessers?" asked Sissy Shirk, trembling.

"Yeah but they couldn't see us," Sal said. "They came bouncing into the EL, and the Guide pushed us out like a whirlwind. She knocked those thugs down."

"We had human miracles, too," Caleb added. "Cynthia and Irving engineered everything: Citadel maps, disabled alarms. You should have seen those Treds running backwards."

"When we got to entrance level, they tripped a power outage," Caleb added. "We literally walked outa there!"

"Jogged," corrected Sal. "We had to jog a couple of kilometers on the dead Tred. Poor Doc Dierk, panting the whole way. He does a lot of walking, but not much running. And he's old. Probably four decades."

"I think Counselor Dred wants to interview you and Irv." Lizzie gave Cynthia a playful tap. "He's got new openings on the Citadel Tech Team."

"Ooooh. Morbid. What happens to failed Yessers?" someone asked.

"Speaking of Dred," Caleb added, "He showed up as we left, and opened the doors for us. He shot at us, but the Guide saved us."

"What about the Wilds tour?" asked Sissy.

Keren flicked her tab. "We've got a few viz of the Wildlings—"

The group gaped at a giant anteater, howler monkey and a leopard conversing with Bopha. "Are you using telepathy?" Lizzie asked. "The viz didn't pick up any words."

"Not sure," Bopha said. Keren snapped off her tab as a Yesser walked by. Bopha switched on hers and thumbed it rapidly.

"Ms. Snooper, do you want to see some leeches?" Bopha offered, smiling sweetly. "They are a real interesting Annelida on my part of the planet." The woman took a peek, grimaced and moved away.

"I guess we'd better get to class," Caleb said. "To sum up: All Ops GO, detainee relocated, sim ready, allies alerted, and the Dominion thwarted."

"But they are still destroying nature," Arana said.

"This is their time," Bopha said.

Chester Noblitts appeared at their table, smirking. "Hey, Nature Heads, look at this."

Chester's dad, Lester Noblitts, a wealthy dealmaker, had a reputation for over-the-top resorts. Chester flicked his tab in Caleb's face and a virtual scene appeared: casitas and swimming pools artfully arranged among pine trees and nestled into a familiar low point between two peaks.

"This is Dad's biggest deal yet: The Saddle Resort at Purity Wild. There's gonna be an Auto transport ribbon direct from City Center to Purity Ridge."

"Not happening, Ches!" Sal corrected. "Large-scale private developments are illegal in the Wilds."

"Guess you haven't read the fine print of the Wilds Development Protocol," Chester corrected. His tab showed *Wilds Development Options Clause: private–public partnerships for exotic public property development are encouraged to improve civilized recreation opportunities in the Wilds system.*

"Wanta read it?" Chester asked.

Caleb shook his head.

"This is the biggest boon in development history," Chester said. "With current tech and expansion prospects, the Bailong Elevator and Ski Dubai will look like tinker toys."

"Enjoy your moment, Techno-head," Marc said. "Nature will fight you."

"Gen-Engineering is the new Nature," Chester retorted. "Wake up, primitives and join the 22nd century." He swaggered away.

No one spoke.

Purity Mountain Wild—the ridge view, the butterscotch smell of warming pine sap, wading in the pools of Sycamore Creek, the singing trees on Sully Saddle. A whirling Auto drowning out the pine song, towering condos consuming Happy Meadow. Appalling.

"Maybe the Wildlings should visit the Noblitts," Lizzie said. "Black bears and cougars could help them experience the Wild."

Keren giggled at visions of black bears investigating the Noblitts' kitchen stores while a cougar joined family members in their "den," plopping herself down on the couch between terrified parents.

"We didn't discuss what they would do when they came to town," she said. "I guess they'll just show up and head for City Center. People haven't seen Wildlings outside of Zo-Parks. Certainly not on the street."

Fourth period chime sounded; the teams dispersed to classes. The last two periods dragged to their merciful end, and everyone went home.

"That is so bizarre that the High Counselor visited your MERC and interviewed the OA Biology class," Nora said. "Old Dierk must have done something radical to get so much attention."

"You had Dr. Dierk for biology, does he strike you as a radical, Nor?" Caleb asked.

"Well it's a little rad to spend all your free time trudging around those Wilds, but nope. He's boring," Nora said. "Did the Dominion kidnap him?"

"I bet the Dominion wants to keep Dr. Dierk incommunicado so they can push the Wilds Protocol through the TRI-WAC," Caleb said.

"I will be so glad when the TRI-WAC is over," Nora sniffed. "All this droning on about world peace and productivity initiatives, the gleaming towers, and smiling delegates in native costumes. And now this stupid Orange Alert," she added. "First they boast about harmony, and then they act like we're fighting a war."

"A war on the Wilds," Caleb said.

"I know it's a pain to be stuck with the fam tonight, Nor," Bill Benson said. "But they'll lift the Orange Alert after delegate departure tomorrow."

"It's the weekend," Nora said. "They moved the games to Saturday to accommodate the Dominion." She scooted out from the table, grabbing her plate and cup. "'Scuse me, I need to get through this pile of homework so I can at least enjoy Saturday. And no, I do *not* want to watch Newsflash."

"So what is the High Counselor like, Caleb? It must be interesting to meet such an important person," Mom said.

"'Interesting' is an understatement, Mom," Caleb said, recalling Dred's fathomless eyes. "He is scary. I don't know how else to put it. There's something dark about him. It makes me wonder about the goals of the Dominion."

"Well, I find it odd that the top security official in this town has time to come to a middle school and question a bunch of kids," Bill Benson said. "The Dominion needs to rein in their staff."

"Maybe we should have a silent moment for Dr. Dierk and for the future of our Wilds," Mom suggested. "I do not trust the Dominion."

Caleb and his parents joined hands and bowed their heads.

The Andersons watched Newsflash. The cams captured the Accelerated Urban Improvement Project in appalling detail—buzzing saws slicing through large trees, giant grapplers swinging them around and dumping sturdy bodies into the chipper's maw, the diggers ripping and tearing the ground.

Tug loved the carnage.

"BUILD, BUILD, BUILD!" he screamed. He sprang from his seat and scurried out. He returned toting a toy excavator, plastic safety helmet tilted on his little head.

"RRRRROOOOM!" He rammed the yellow plastic crane into Keren's chair. "Knock it down! Rip it up!" He tried to clamp the crane claw around the chair leg.

"Stop that!" Keren yelled. "Mother!"

"Hey Tugger, let's build a reservoir in the bathroom," said Dad. He grabbed the excavator in one hand and swung the toddler to his shoulder with the other. "Rrrrrrrrrr! Boom! Boom! Let's get your laser shovel, Tug. We can dig, dig, dig."

"Riparian improvement project, Dad?" Keren quipped as the pair headed through the door.

"Yes, we'll build a dam, a reservoir, generate power, stop unregulated flooding and provide recreation opportunities," the angular artist said as he headed for the stairs. "Another engineering win-win."

She heard Dad's voice echoing down from the upstairs bathroom. "After we make the lake, do you want to swim or take out the boats?"

"Simmm, simm, boat, boat!" She heard the high voice, tricked by Dad's "engineering" a bath.

Dad is good, she thought. Patient as a tree. No artsy-fartsy temperament. He channels his creativity into managing Tug's energy. I wonder how he "manages" me? She vaguely recalled "Little Panther" stories focused on her childish traumas; in one, the panther kept changing her outfits and missed a park outing.

Keren longed to tell her parents about the Keeper's project to save the Wilds. The thought of an awed Tug in the presence of a real Big Cat made her smile. She could see the Keeper's feline image, golden eyes and giant paws, the great tail lashing to the rhythm of the Great Dance. *Soon, soon, my love, we will dance again in the wild joy of life.*

She left Mother watching Small Business News and headed upstairs to work on Mincer's annoying OA Biology homework. Teachers and Yessers—two different species.

chapter twenty
WILD VISITORS

C aleb woke early Saturday morning, surprised at the silence. No blowers. No whackers. Not even the whisk of Auto ribbons. The curfew banned urban activity. Had the delegates departed?

He grabbed his wrist tab and aimed at the monitor across the room. AM Newsflash erupted on the screen.

"Air launch will commence in one kilosecond," said newscaster Fred Flaky from the Citadel roof. Behind him, suited delegates filed into the open door of a gleaming transworld rocket.

"This XX-70 will remove our delegates to the rocket launch facility for secure takeoff into orbit," Flaky said. "Total transport time including shuttles, orbit, and reentry is about 15 kiloseconds. All delegates will arrive at Del Palace around 2400 Babel I continental time, 30 kiloseconds before TRI-WAC Opening Ceremonies on Sunday."

Caleb hopped out of bed. He donned his running suit and foot pads. Curfew would lift once the delegates launched. Caleb wanted to get in a long training run. He planned to hit the closest parks to observe the effects of Friday's Accelerated Improvement Project.

His parents banged around the kitchen, Newsflash droning as background noise. He bounded downstairs.

"Anxious for the delegates' launch, Cal?" asked Dad.

"I can hardly wait," Caleb said. "I've felt like a cooped-up cougar the past hundred kilosecs. Indoor laps on the Sim Track can't match an outdoor run. I would rather jog a block outside than five miles on a fake beach."

"There are just so many real things that cannot be simulated," his mother said, "despite what society thinks."

CRACK! BAM! BAM! Fireworks sounded from the monitor and echoed through the outside pane. The city roared with simulated joy.

"Another chapter of world progress begins!" Flaky hollered over the din.

"Security curfew hereby lifted. Safe travels, venerated delegates," said the Chief Commissioner, flanked by Security Counselor Dred. The politician beamed and Dred grimaced—the clown and his death angel.

The screen divided into four frowning faces representing the Green Coalition, the Park Preservation League, the Nature Appreciation Society and the Urban Exercise Club. "As Babel leadership celebrated a successful delegate launch, other leaders are not so pleased," said newscaster Flaky. "Now we hear from the opposition to new development proposals."

"We are saddened and disturbed by yesterday's violent acts against our parks and green areas in Babel II," said Nat Geo, Green president. "Accelerated Urban Improvement is an unwarranted display of power by the Dominion Human Security. The progressive movement seeks to destroy nature. Their wanton destruction of parks sets the scene for enacting the proposed Wild Development Protocol."

"The people of Babel II do *not* support this proposal of destruction, regardless of the pabulum our leaders are feeding us," added Delilah Wilder, director of the Park Preservation League. "We urge everyone to join us at 1200 today at the ruins of the Puddicombe Pocket Park for the Save Our Wilds Demonstration."

Bold words, legally permitted and totally disregarded by the Dominion. Speak the truth, friends. Sunday you will be heard.

"I'm headed out, Mom," Caleb called over his shoulder. "See ya in about five kilosecs."

"Be careful, Caleb," his mother said.

Cal jogged through the sleepy city. Autos started to whir, signs lit with shopping specials and Sim ads beckoned Auto travelers. He trotted below the din and lights. Ad-market reach didn't consider pedestrians. Fine with him.

He reached the new temp fencing on the perimeter of Puddicombe Nature Park. Trees had been chipped into neat piles for transport to a paper processor in the Far West Industrial Sector. A new asphalt path wound along through spindly Gen trees planted in orderly rows, one meter high, designed for controlled growth. Green turf had been laid out along a straightened creek. A hovercraft lowered a security arch before a new double gate in the temp fence for weapons check, a standard protocol for large demonstrations.

Caleb found other pocket parks along his 19K ramble in earlier, uglier stages of transformation. Temp fences up, orders posted, and chaos created: nothing left but felled trees, flattened terrain, watery pits, rock piles, and rolled-up turf mounds. Pots of Gen trees awaited planting.

"Hey son, this is a Public Improvement Zone," a Security Yesser called as Cal peered through the fence at the ruined South-Central Park. "For your own personal safety, please move on."

Caleb eyed the blue-uniformed guard in his little bunker. It figured. Security Yessers on overtime pay for TRI-WAC weekend. Caleb's favorite trail through the desert forest of South-Central: ruined. Nothing natural left. Perhaps he preferred the sim track after all; at least you could project a beautiful natural environment from the past. Soon we will need nature museums.

I'll do my training runs in the Desert Wild, he thought. Notions of bounding along desert hills with Coati, the Cougar and a mule deer made him smile. He looked skyward and offered a request before vacating the park wreckage and loping home.

Keren rose early for a head start on OA Biology homework. She had promised to go to the SOW demo, but the rest of her weekend she reserved for the Keeper's plans. She'd support the demonstrators; at least they stood up against the system.

She heard the fireworks outside and chatter from the monitor downstairs. Oh yeah. The delegate departure. No escaping that fiasco.

"Breakfast, Keren," Mother called up.

"Let me finish this one exercise." She tabbed off the homework and headed down.

They all snarfed pancakes. Tug chomped on a banana, eyes glued to the monitor. Mother had switched from Newswatch to cartoons. Better plot line than what the Dominion put out.

"Can you and the kids handle the Farmer's Market?" Mother asked Dad. "I'll open the shop. We can meet up at Puddicombe."

"Hey Tugboat, time for the market," Dad said. "If you get dressed quick, we'll have time to visit the petting zoo."

Tug shifted from starship commander to farmer and hurried off to find his overalls. "Wanta drive tractor," he said.

"In space or out, it's always about machines for Tug," Keren said.

"It's always about machines for most small boys, Keren," Mother said. "But some grow up to be like your friend Caleb."

Mother picked up her work bag and headed for the AUTO, skipping her usual morning walk.

Keren put a wrap and water bottle into her go-bag. She didn't know when the Keeper would call her. Best to be prepared.

She returned to Mincer's project: comparing 10 biological classification schemes ranging from Linnaeus in 1735 to Cavalier-Smith in the 1990s and Squirrel et al. in 2035 in exacting detail—busywork. Precision and detail should be tools in science, not ends in themselves. But Yessers confused this distinction.

If we win, Dr. Dierk returns and we skip this "pop quiz," she considered. Only a detail freak like Irv or Jenna with her eidetic memory excelled at rote memorization. Pointless, since info streamed on every wrist tab. Why don't they just implant a memory chip? That would free up time for creative inference and wonder.

Keren, Dad and Tug joined the sea of people moving with slow determination into Puddicombe Park. Attendees entered through a scanner archway. Periodically, a belt or other metallic accessory would trip the "weapon" alarm, WHEEEEEEEE-WHEEEEEEE. A Yesser escorted the offender offside and waved a detector to find and confiscate the article. The owner then reentered the arch. A beepless crossing cleared the demonstrator to join the throng.

After three hectoseconds of growing mobs queuing before the arch, an air cruiser settled near the entrance. Security Yessers disembarked, carrying parts for a second arch. After a hectosecond of assembly, the line began to move through the new arch, ending the bottleneck.

Keren felt relief. Dad had checked Tug for "weapons" before they left. The little boy had had his Military Assault Rifle hanging out of a belt holster, a toy blaster in a pocket and a stash of explosive mini-rockets bulging in a little bag stuffed under his tunic top. She recalled stories of children suspended for bringing a toy weapon to school. Who knew what Tug's artillery could incite. Dad made him leave his armaments at home.

"No weapons, Tug," Dad said. "This is a peaceful gathering."

"You said march," said Tug. "Need weapons for march."

"I think he watched some twentieth century military parades," Keren said. "This is a peaceful gathering, Tug. Peace march. No tanks. No rockets. No guns."

Tug had a bright future as a Security Yesser. They shared his fascination for noisy toys and military maneuvers. As they waited their turn at the arch, Tug wriggled. Only Dad's friendly but firm hand on his shoulders kept him in line. Keren feared he would dart out to "help soljers" at any minute.

"Maybe I should have stayed home with Tugger," she whispered to her father.

"I didn't want you both cooped up in the house all day," Dad replied. "We all need to get outside, breathe some real air—until the Dominion figures out how to replace it with something engineered and metered."

They moved smoothly through the security arch, to Tug's disappointment and Keren's great relief. The crowd milled around the new park amphitheater, hundreds seated and others standing on arti-sod. Hot sun beat on her head. The new leaf-off Gen trees provided little shade.

A playground to the side offered the children an exercise alternative to whining and tantrums. They slid, swung or bounced on antigravitation equipment. "Tug, look, there's a satellite." Keren pointed towards the Anti-Grav.

Tug turned from eyeing Security Yessers to the playground. "Go fly spacesip Da?" he asked.

"I can keep an eye on Tug," Keren said. Dad left and went off to look for Mother.

Released, Tug sprang for the Anti-Grav, and started bouncing and shouting with other youngsters in the transparent cube.

Keren leaned against a Gen tree and tuned in to voices from the center stage. Lines had dispersed, the amphitheater had filled and a small crowd had gathered around the perimeter.

"Welcome, Wild Lovers and citizen supporters of naturalness," she heard in Nat Geo's measured tones. "We apologize for the delay. The Dominion requested security precheck for all participants. The large crowd and limited security portal created a traffic bottleneck. But we are proud of the large numbers supporting our Wild places. Not all Babelites support unbridled development!" he shouted.

The crowd roared agreement. "GO NAT! SAVE OUR WILDS! DOWN WITH THE DOMINION! DOWN WITH DEVELOP-MENT!"

Geo raised his hands, hushing the hubbub. "Let's listen to the voices of dissent."

Delilah Wilder tearfully chronicled the week's park destruction disasters. Keren caught a flash of viz images and a collective OHHHHHHHH from park lovers—probably projecting the carnage of toppled trees and flattened forests. Someone from Anti-Development League gave a detailed diatribe on the carnage to be unleashed under the Wilds Development Protocol.

"Towers atop the Himalaya Wilds," she heard followed by shouts of "NO! NO! NO!" Then "here's the New Atlantis Undersea Resort—trashing the last reaches of Ocean Wilds." Keren just couldn't bring herself to move closer and see Ms. Wilder's visual displays. Painful.

Soon Dr. Geo spoke again. "Let me introduce our distinguished panel of natural scientists to explain the grave consequences of the proposed protocol on processes of the earth and atmosphere."

Stirring speeches and sober science. But what did they accomplish? They sputtered and warned while the Dominion rolled on like an army tank in one of Tug's beloved war viz.

Keren heard excerpts, "Wilds purify water and air system...necessary baseline of naturalness...unknown long-term effects for engineered environments...biological diversity."

Behind the speakers' panel, official Dominion Guest Listeners sat in a row. She could not see their faces but envisioned them listening attentively, nodding and clapping politely at presenter points. They could absolutely not care less.

Oh yeah, the Dominion is happy to listen and to record our concerns. Public participation directives meticulously followed. Newsflash will show flics of shouting speakers, the roaring crowd, and thousands marching on the Citadel, raising their puny fists against the Powers.

This afternoon Babel PR will issue an official summary of SOW concerns and Dominion point-by-point response, available to every HEAD and tab, immediately analyzed on Newsflash. Noreen Nose will quiz the Commissioner. He'll offer a thoughtful response, his trademark twinkle, a joke, a promise. Citizen dissent heard, summarized, provided to all interested publics, answered and dismissed.

"The Keeper is right," she thought. "Only in experiencing the Wilds is there a chance for change. Facts and predictions do not move hearts."

Screams interrupted Keren's reverie. She looked back to the playground and saw Tug, another small boy, and a feisty little girl wrestling for the toy "control board" of the Anti-Grav chamber.

"I am Captain Kirk, Star Fleet Commander!" the little girl, older and taller than Tug, screamed shrilly. She tried to pry Tug's grip off the toy shifter. The other boy screamed mindlessly and made fists at his rival, offering a male alternative to solve the command issue.

"Commander Tug!" Keren hurried into the playground. "Admiral Anderson wants you at Star Fleet Headquarters. Disengage from the conflict. I repeat, disengage!"

Tug sputtered but let go, leaving the shifter to his rivals. He floated to the entrance.

Mother and Dad joined Keren at the Anti-Grav entrance, drawn by familiar screams.

"Someone is getting a little tired," Mother murmured as a tearful Tug emerged. She picked him up and held him close.

"I can take Tug home, Mom," Keren said. Sad and bored with fruitless proceedings, she wanted to escape, even if it meant Tug-tending. Her overstimulated little brother would be ready for a nap. She could finish her silly homework.

The speakers finished and participants gathered for the March on the Citadel.

"That's very thoughtful," Mother said. "Admiral Keren, please accompany the starship commander to home port." Hmm, who had higher rank than the Admiral? Mother must be the Commander In Chief.

"I don't think Tug will thrive on the 4K SOW March," Dad agreed.

"Commander Tug, dismissed!" Mother snapped, setting the toddler on his feet. She and Dad gave brief salutes to their children, returned snappily by Commander Tug and half-heartedly by Admiral Keren.

"Yes Ma'am, Command- uh, Mother," Keren said. "C'mon Commander, let's march to the Auto," Keren told Tug. "Hup to, hup to, hup to, hup..."

Waving back at her parents, she goose-stepped away, matching Tug's short steps as they marched through the arch and headed for the Auto station. "Home port, Commander Tug."

Back home, her Star Song for sleepy Tug ended mid-note.

"*Star Angel!*" screamed Tug, and sat up on his pallet, instantly awake and pointing at the luminous Guide lighting up his room.

Oh no, thought Keren. Now what? The Call arrived, and she had a three-year-old on her hands.

Dred exulted in another smooth TRI-WAC convention departure. Sometimes technology performed as expected, barring human incompetence. His special security force monitored the SOW Demonstration, and a few undercover Yessers had joined the march as credible Greenies in their sandals and tunics.

Meanwhile reports from other Babels indicated orderly delegate transport and all delegates now resting in their quarters.

Dred expected the usual high honors and pay bonus. His personal keepers also seemed satisfied. He needed to keep it that way through the TRI-WAC. Then he could enjoy a week's R&R at a luxurious retreat on a small tropical island. Dred had applied for benefits under the Scenic Privatization Protocol passed at the very first TRI-WAC.

He leaned back, gazing at walls plastered with awards and photos of Dred posing with Commissioners and viz stars. He never imagined such success as a young security engineer in Dominion Human Security.

At the buzz on his wrist tab, the High Counselor gave a start.

"Sir, we have some reports from the West Desert Gate," he heard.

"Give me a viz."

The office monitor filled with Wildlings. Wildlings pouring out of Desert Wild through the West Gate. Flipping for close up, Dred saw deer, coyotes, bobcats and cougars bounding through the gate. Coatimundis scurried, tails waving like banners. He panned a ground view of javelinas, jackrabbits, field mice and lizards scampering along at the hooves and paws of the larger animals. Roadrunners and quail scurried among the throng. Rattlesnakes, flipping end over end like leeches, appeared to roll like wheels. Cactus wrens, woodpeckers, flickers and thrashers flew above the horde; tiny hummingbirds whirred among them. Dred flicked on sound: a cacophony of roars, growls, howls, grunts, chirps and screams.

The ground Wildlings passed a stunned group of Rangers and Peripheral Security Yessers. Once through the gate, the company split into sections, each following a different arterial into the central city.

"Orders, sir? Should we intercept and destroy?"

Destroying Wildlings, a satisfying thought, with hordes of life obliterated in a few white flashes. But the creatures had already moved into Far West Industrial Sector, trains and auto-trucks halting as operators gaped in amazement. Illegally obliterating protected species would enrage the Nature Heads, already out on the streets for their march. They just needed an excuse to riot.

Current law protected Wildlings. Not for long. The Wild Development Protocol would delist Wildlings; they could be exterminated like any other urban pest. But not yet. He had no legal tools to manage or remove Wildlings.

Dred panned his observer-cams, following the Wildling progress through the city. Industrial operations had stopped; workers poured out of warehouses to stand gaping at the parade. Few had ever seen Wildlings. Tame Zo animals, pets and a few birds and squirrels were all that they knew of Wildlings. Until now.

"Urban security protection force—hold fire. Alert traffic control to initiate emergency slow-down protocols. Redirect Auto to mini-mize collisions. Initiate Red/Orange Alert and deploy forces to these parades. Do not fire on Wildlings, unless they injure someone. Be the good guys here."

Another tab buzz. "Sir, we have reports of Wildling movement into all principle Babels and some secondary cities," his world security officer reported.

"Give me viz, Mort," said Dred.

The vision of desert Wildlings melted into black and reconstituted as a scene from a simulated wildlife safari on steroids. Giant pandas, tigers and monkeys padded into Babel V.

"Pan the other incursions," Dred said.

For the next two kiloseconds, Dred sat appalled as his monitor provided shows beyond the wildest dreams of the Wildlife Entertainment Network: Bengal tigers, lions, elephants, barking deer and macaws and monkeys entering Babel II 2.2; jaguars, deer, coatis and anteaters streaming out of the rainforest into other urban areas.

Near the coastal cities, large schools of fish, and pods of whales, sharks, and dolphins swam around the bays and up the transport waterways; herds of seals and penguin colonies waddled through the outskirts of "Baby Babels" (metropolitan areas not yet Babel population size). Every Wild within 100 kilometers of human habitation sent delegates to visit humanity. Impounded Wildlings had somehow escaped their Zo-Parks to join their counterparts moving towards city centers.

From some of the more remote Wilds, air monitors displayed giant flying reptiles, matching a description recalled from the Desert Wild Visitation incident Thursday morning. Staff paleontologists had identified them from Yesser descriptions and the mind-sim reproductions: Quetzalcoatlus, extinct a hundred million years ago.

The flying lizards ferried Wildlings from the Celestial, Himalayan and other remote mountain Wilds to city limits. Air drone monitors captured viz of snow leopards, mountain goats, roe deer, boars, bears, antelopes, gazelles and hamsters perched within the whomping wings as golden eagles, pigeons, choughs, crows and vultures flew alongside in formation. The giant reptiles set down at the gates of municipalities, unfurling their wings as ramps for their living cargo to move onto the city streets. With a hop, they launched into the air, and vanished from the monitors.

Dred's console lit up with alarms; counterparts across the world calling in. What should they do? Worldwide military forces deployed. But no aggressive action permitted. DHS and Urban Transport Authority in every Babel tried to manage traffic chaos as thousands of riders simultaneously reprogrammed STOP on their Auto route for a view of Wildlings. Shoppers, partiers, sports fans, families on outing stopped and leaned off the stalled ribbons to gape. People poured out of homes and stood on turf as Wildlings paraded by. Most of the world's cities came to a stop, their inhabitants watching the Wildlings come to town.

Of course, only the western half of the world watched the Wildlings. In the Far Eastern reaches of Babel I and IV, where citizens slept in the wee hours of Sunday morning, quiet reigned. Morning cleaners and sweepers, the only humans awake, gaped at Wildlings entering their cities.

"What's going on? Why are we stopping?" Cheryl Anderson asked. Save our Wilds marchers had stopped a kilometer short of the Citadel. A buzz went up. Phil Anderson strained to see beyond the agitated crowd.

Suddenly, the confusion and questioning turned to joyful whoops. "Wildlings!" someone screamed, followed by stunned silence.

The Save our Wilds Demonstration had been joined. Walkers slowed to allow throngs of cougars, coyotes, javelinas and other desert-dwellers to merge with their ranks from several adjoining arterials. Wildlings and humans walked together towards the City Center.

I wish Keren could see this, her mother thought.

chapter twenty-one
WILD DELEGATES

Keren found a warming cloak for Tug and put it on him. "The Star Angel will take us on a mission," she said. What else could she do? She couldn't leave Tug home alone. He'd wander the streets seeking the "Star Angel."

Why had the Guide come so early? she wondered. Oh yeah. She forgot the math, as usual. Babel I 1.1 time zone ran 10 HEX hours (15 hours traditional measure) ahead—0600 Sunday already there. Wow.

The Guide waited through her preparations, apparently unconcerned about the extra passenger. Keren had hoped the being might wave a hand or a wand and put Tug to sleep. Come to think of it, the Keeper always welcomed children and even scolded followers who tried to hinder their access.

Soon they hurtled through bright corridors. Tug screamed in delight. Keren held him tight within the Guide's presence as they flew across time and space.

In Babel I 1.1, workers at the Exalted Urban Extravaganza Centre (fondly called the "EU") made final preparations for the TRI-WAC Convention opening: light shows, fireworks and a dizzying visual display of worldwide development triumphs. Exotic aromas wafted through the waking city. The EU grounds encompassed 10 square kilometers in a layout of ponds, rockworks, forests and floral gardens. Its meeting halls and pavilions were linked by winding paths through traditional gardens. Babel I 1.1 valued history and tradition over the all-out progressivism of its sister cities. At the EU center, the Great Tower rose to staggering heights topped by the Hall of Meeting, made of transparent alumina. The shift to fusion power decades past had cleared the city skies. The transparent Tower offered astounding views of the sprawling city surrounded by verdant hills. Babel I 1.1 gave testimony to the benefits of urbanization.

A few kilometers from the EU, early morning walkers and exerdancers stopped and gaped at giant pandas, Siberian tigers, zebras, yaks, red foxes, boars and camels moving along the riverfront towards the EU at City Center. A panda made a little dance move as he passed, waving his paws.

One by one, Guides collected Dierk's students, and moved them to the EU on the other side of the planet.

A few had glimpsed Wildling visitors processing past their homes, or picked up by a Newsflash broadcast, before their summons. The diversion helped a circumspect getaway.

Bopha was glad her large family was distracted by the Wildlings. Everyone had poured out of the house into Uncle Devi's front yard to gape at javelinas, jackrabbits and foxes bounding down the rarely used street. Bopha felt a presence around her; then she moved rapidly and soundlessly away from her family to another gathering on the other side of the earth.

Dr. Dierk and his students found themselves in the midst of the grove of Super Trees, living towers of ferns, vines, orchards and tropical flowering plants. The Guides surrounded them as a radiant cloud of energy and light: a great company of beings, blinding brightness of concentrated Presence. The beings gazed lovingly at their human charges, then faded away, leaving them in the dimmer light of dawn.

Dr. Dierk embraced his mob of joyous students. "Dr. Dierk!" screamed Lizzie.

"Shhhh," he said. "The security here is intense. I am sure that's why the Guides deposited us out in the gardens."

Tug stared wide-eyed at the Super Trees. Keren wondered how long he would be quiet.

"This is my little brother Theodore; we call him 'Tug,'" she said. "Believe me, Dr. Dierk, I did *not* plan to bring him, but the Guide caught me by surprise and I couldn't leave him alone."

"Hello Tug, thank you for joining our secret mission." The teacher smiled at the toddler. "If the Guide came for Tug, we must need him."

Keren seriously doubted this.

"Can you stand by me, Agent Tug, and be quiet as a spy?" Dr. Dierk asked. "We need to discuss our mission."

Tug nodded, eyes still wide and mind dazzled by his "warp speed" trip and new surroundings. Still clinging to Keren's hand, he moved closer to Dr. Dierk.

The teacher gestured towards the ground and the little group sat down on emerald green turf.

"Fill me in, troops," Dr. Dierk said. "Have the Wildlings shown up? Have you located the essential human coordinates for the sim projections?"

Yes and yes, they told him. Cynthia discovered a Dominion Security pathway perfect for projecting the Wilds Simulation and identifying the audience.

"The Security Cyber Access Project pretty well links to all HEAD users to monitor the populace for potentially subversive actions," Cynthia noted. "Once we hacked the SCAP we had access to anyone who is a frequent HEAD user—about 95 percent of the population."

"Cal sent me your Wild Projection improvements and I synced them right into the simulator," Marc said. "I have a link right here on my tab."

"Great work," Dr. Dierk said. "Now we need to find the Hall of Meeting and set up a remote transmit into their projection unit."

Irving fiddled with his own tab a minute and grinned. "Remote is available. Marc, just flick your wrist my way." With a buzz, an arc of light shot between the two wrist tabs.

"All you have to do is point your wrist at their projection unit, once we're in the chamber," Irving said. "But how do we get there?"

"I don't know," Dr. Dierk admitted. "Can anyone queue up a ground map of the EU?" Tabs tapped and a virtual map projected. "The Tower where the TRI-WAC meets is about 1 km away," Arana said.

"It's 0730 now and the convention opening ceremony is 0800. We'd better move," Dr. Dierk said. He swung Tug up on his shoulder and the group scurried along garden paths towards the Great Tower and the Hall of Meeting.

At the edge of the gardens, they stopped at a "green wall" 2.5 meters high, covered with shrubbery. Arana noted a set of dangling vines and immediately swung her way to the top.

"How do you expect us mortals to follow you, Spiderwoman?" asked Sal.

"Aw come on, guys, don't you recall the teamwork wall climb maneuver from Phys Ed?" Arana noted. "Dr. Dierk, Cal, you're the support guys."

They built a human pyramid and teammates climbed up to shoulders where Arana helped them over the wall to swing down and drop quietly on the other side. Dr. Dierk and Caleb handed Tug up to Keren who waited on top, holding the spellbound child. Dierk and Caleb made their way up, holding the vines and "walking" up the brushy surface. After Dierk dropped down, Keren gently handed Tug down to her teacher and swung down to the ground.

They stood in the shadow of shrubs along the wall, gazing at the Great Tower. Delegates trooped inside, ringed by a human wall of Babel I 1.1 Security Yessers. Each passed through a security arch, which buzzed as it recognized IDs.

"See that light on top of the arch?" Irving whispered. "That's a dual entrance-security device. If your ID isn't recognized, it sends out a radiation ray that inflicts major burns."

"I think the TRI-WAC takes this 'membership only' status a little too seriously!" Lizzie whispered. "You're either in the club—or you're dead!"

"Irving and Cynthia, could you disable that ray gun and create a distraction in the Meeting Hall?" Dr. Dierk asked.

"On it, Dr. D.," the pair replied, heads bent over their tabs, programming furiously.

All at once the soaring chamber a thousand meters above them filled with roars, flashes and small explosions. The simulated fireworks extravaganza had started prematurely. The security arch crackled and buzzed, its light flickered and went dead.

"All Hands Alert!" a loudspeaker roared. Security Yessers pushed ahead of the line of delegates, rushing into the Tower to confront an assumed terrorist attack on the TRI-WAC. The Yessers gently moved remaining dignitaries to the side of the line.

In the chaos, Dr. Dierk and his students lined up behind the Yessers, hoping to slip inside during the distraction.

Then Tug suddenly wailed. "Need baffroom, Keren, need to go *now!*" he cried.

To everyone's horror, Yessers in the queue looked back. "Trespass alert!" barked one. Several Yessers surrounded the teacher and students.

"How did you people get into the complex?" the Security Yesser-in-Charge (SYC) asked. "Take them to the holding compound," she ordered.

Looking at the grim guards with stunners drawn, Dr. Dierk and his forces quietly surrendered. "Take prisoner?" asked Tug. "Fight! Fight!" he screamed, trying to loosen Keren's grip on his hand.

"Hey little warrior, go with your friends," said the grinning SYC. "I won't pulverize a child."

Yessers marched the TRI-WAC invaders to a nearby Interloper Holding Compound and told them to sit on a row of benches along the wall. Keren heard strains of triumphant music drifting down from the nearby tower. The TRI-WAC, only briefly delayed by their diversion, had begun.

The amused SYC led Keren and her brother to a public lavatory on one side of the compound. Inside the facility, Keren sighed as the youngster did his business and almost forgot the required response, "Good job, Tug!"

Good job indeed. Confined, arrested as trespassers with the International DHS even now checking their IDs against an international roster. In a kilosecond, Dr. Dierk would be tagged as a suspect in a TRI-WAC disruption plot and an escapee from high-security detention, packed off to prison and then tried for international high treason against urbanity. They would be in trouble, too. And they had lost their chance to save the Wilds.

She knew TRI-WAC had scheduled a presentation on the Wild Development Protocol right after the Opening Exercises. How could they possibly get to the convention chambers and beam the Wild Projection to those delegates first?

"Don't worry, Keren," Dr. Dierk said as she ushered Tug back to join the dejected team on the benches. "The Keeper's timing is perfect. Disaster almost always precedes success."

Something crashed outside; everyone ran for the windows. Green walls separating the Tower from the conference grounds fell in sections. A great sound like a hundred trumpets combined with several loud sneezes filled the air.

Two dozen elephants trooped through the grounds, shouldering the walls down as they came.

Keren knew that Quetzacoatlus had brought them from Stone Forest Wild, a distant 900K away and too far for a walk. Behind the elephants bounded other members of the Wild delegation: tigers, clouded leopards, snow leopards, jaguars, giant pandas, sloths, macaques, gibbons, yaks and others native to the Babel I continent, following the pachyderms towards the Tower. A pair of pandas stopped at the doors of the Interloper Holding Compound and easily tore them open.

"Come!" called a large Tiger Who stood between the pandas at the doorway.

"It's the Keeper!" Keren and Caleb cried in unison. The Tiger bounded through the door. He stared calmly at the stunned Yessers. As He gazed into each face, the guards quietly reholstered their weapons. "Children of men, it is time to listen, not to destroy," He announced. "Come with us to the great chambers and hear the truth."

He motioned with a great paw to Tug and crouched down low. "Come, ride on My back, child. We will lead the procession." The wide-eyed Tug clambered obediently onto the Tiger's broad back.

The Tiger strode to the head of the waiting Wildlings, followed by Dr. Dierk and the students. Behind them, scores of animals marched, followed by dazed Security Yessers.

The security arch stood disabled. The throng entered the Great Tower. Since the elephants could not fit in the ELs, the animals headed for the emergency stairs and bounded up the winding stairway towards the top floor. Empowered by the Keeper, everyone leaped and bounded rapidly ever upwards towards the Meeting Hall, where human decisions would impact the future of the planet and its remnant Wilds.

Within the meeting hall, the Opening Exercises drew to a close. A multiscreen presentation highlighted several Babels and their diverse human populations. It profiled mega-developments such as the Babel III Banking Complex, the Babel I Hydro-Mega-Dam, and the Indoor Reservoir Recreation Complex in Babel VII—where people swam, boated and sunbathed under artificial solar lights in a hot-spring-heated subterranean complex beneath melting remains of the polar ice cap.

Suddenly the screens went blank and the chamber doors flew open. Trumpeting of elephants announced the new arrivals. Wildlings entered the chambers, led by an enormous Tiger ridden by a small boy. The delegates broke into wild applause.

"This is the greatest simulation I've ever experienced," whispered a Babel II delegate to her counterpart. "You can even smell the elephants!"

They think this is part of the special effects, Keren mused. The air filled with the musty scent of a thousand Wildlings—something never before experienced in the highly engineered atmosphere of urbanity. Something earthy and alive on a scale beyond imagination. The Wilds had come to civilization.

The delegates had filled the chamber, designed as a semi-circle facing the stage. Wildlings walked up the center row. Smaller Wildlings such as gibbons, macaques, langurs, lorises and sand lizards took seats in the back while the larger animals moved to the front of the room and began to line the front walls.

The Tiger moved to the podium, where the moderator stood, gaping. The large beast bowed low to the moderator in proper Babel I courtesy (with Tug hanging on for dear life to the fur of His neck). Surprised, the moderator returned the bow, turned on his heel and walked back to his seat in a front row.

The Tiger opened His mouth in a roar that shook the chamber. At the same time Keren distinctly heard, "Peace to you, friends! We bring a message from the Wilds of your world." From looks of recognition around the room, some delegates and all of Dr. Dierk's entourage heard His words; others heard only a terrifying roar.

The Tiger beckoned with a large paw, and Dr. Dierk joined Him at the podium, followed by the biology class who sat on the stage behind them. The Tiger sat back on large haunches. Tug slid off and sat between the beast's paws.

Dr. Dierk waved his wrist at the screens and a new scene unfolded—the mountainous Wilds just north of Babel I 1.1—with stunning rocky ridges and forests of red pine, oak, and maple. The cam panned across a grove of flowering Golden rain trees, and zooming in, found the furtive figure of a golden cat moving through the understory (vegetation below the tree canopy).

The Wild filled the delegates' HEADs with the fragrance of spring flowers and the fresh sharp smell of mountain air.

Keren knew that these sights, sounds and smells invaded the senses of anyone on earth wearing a HEAD—even if they had not tuned in for the TRI-WAC. Cynthia's bootlegged security pathway overrode all regular programming.

At the back, the Security Yessers stood at attention, entranced.

"Esteemed delegates, leaders of the world, citizens of the earth: we come on behalf of the Wilds," Dr. Dierk said. "The Keeper of Wilds and of all life has asked us to remind you of the life and life-support systems entrusted to us on this planet."

As he spoke, the large screens and HEAD projections swept through scenes of great mountains, tropical forests, grasslands, roaring rivers, deserts and beaches, each time zooming in to explore an area up close with an array of trees, brush, flowering plants and grasses. Wildlings leaped, crept, climbed, crouched, paddled, perched and flew within and above the Wilds. From great to small the story moved: the green stems of lotus plants rose out of murky waters, opening to elegant flowers of pink and orange; a bright orange salamander wound its way along a forest floor.

For the first time in many months, Keren pulled a HEAD from her travel pack and put it on. Her colleagues did the same. They wanted the whole show.

She immediately realized a marked difference between this experience and the many wonderful presentations on Wildlings and Wild habitat most people had watched on *Natural Ways, Raw Wilds* and *Undersea Journeys*. Thanks to Dr. Dierk's all-senses simulations, participants experienced more than a projection and sound: they also roamed through the tropical forest, felt the spongy earth under their feet and the humidity on their skin, and felt breathless in the thin sharp air of a mountain.

The feel of a sultry tropic breeze, the arctic air, sandy ground beneath feet, or the brush of leaves accompanied each experience. Visiting the Ocean Wilds included the bounding lurch of a turbo-ship across the waves of a channel and a dive deep into a submarine canyon to gape at bright colored fish and plants living two km below the surface.

It's Dr. Dierk's capstone, Keren thought. Twenty years of exploring, describing and conveying the Wilds in simulated experience. So few have experienced the Wilds. Until now.

After generations of taming, isolating, and protecting/avoiding the Wilds, Wilds had come to humankind on every level of sight, sound, smell and conception.

"Our modern medical miracles come from plants provided by the Wilds," Dr. Dierk said. "Wilds also help purify the air and water we use." Behind him a trickling stream grew to a large river, cascading off a mountain and culminating in a quiet reservoir.

"Our ancestors lived in the Wilds—their home," Dr. Dierk said.

Now they moved quietly through a dark primeval forest of towering trees. A roar shook the forest and large paws echoed on the ground. Keren felt simple awe, fear and wonder. How would it be to live fully and fearfully in a world crammed with danger and glory?

"Wilds are a reminder of the larger world given to humans to care for and use," Dierk said. "We need to keep them as representative of a better world, one that was and is to come.

"We speak for the Wilds," Dr. Dierk concluded. "But we also speak for humanity itself. We cannot live separate from the natural world. We made an artificial world. We did this remarkably well. But apart from the natural, something in us dies.

"You will soon hear a proposal to develop the remaining Wilds," Dr. Dierk said. "It makes great economic sense—but economics alone will rob us of what makes us human, what makes us truly alive. We are creatures that can create new realities—but we are also creatures of earth."

Dr. Dierk looked to his students. "These young people know the Wilds better than most. They helped create this simulation. They will live out the results of your decisions at this convention. I'd like you to hear from them."

Two years of OA Biology and Wilds study were summed up in a few important moments. Students spoke of personal Wild experience—accompanied by a personal sim. Keren described her first ascent to Purity Mountain Wild, looking down at hills grading into the sprawl of Babel II, the butterscotch scent and wind song of pines.

"My sissa!" screamed Tug, eliciting a loud burst of laughter from the delegates and a sharp stab of embarrassment for Keren. At least he had been absorbed in the simulation and blessedly quiet during her talk.

Caleb took them to Desert Wild, and Bopha ranged through the great red-bark giant dipterocarp trees of Tropical Forest Wild for a close encounter with a rowdy pair of mango-eating monkeys.

"I want my children and their children to experience what I have touched and tasted, to know the great forests where their ancestors lived, hunted and prospered," Bopha said. "To see and smell the resin trees, to stand within the fluted roots of the forest giants. Please do not take our heritage away from us."

Paul Wonk gave the final presentation, on policy. "Honored TRI-WAC delegates, we apologize for our unauthorized visit," he began. "But according to Article 17 of the Worldwide Governance and Peace Proclamation, 'Deliberations for all new Protocols will include full disclosure and discussion of pertinent facts, intelligence and information.' Also, 'All impacted publics will be fully informed and engaged in Protocols that impact their well-being.'

"The key set of facts, intelligence and information missing from previous Wilds Development Protocol deliberations was a full experience of the World Wilds System. Our humble simulation offered this experience," Wonk said.

Keren saw Tug squirming a bit in his seat between the Tiger paws. The Tiger gave his hair a rough lick and the child settled down.

"Wildlings assembled here represent some of the major publics who will be greatly impacted by the passage of the Wild Development Protocol," Wonk added. "As good students, we have tried to help TRI-WAC delegates complete the homework."

After a thoughtful silence, the hall filled with laugher and thunderous applause.

Keren, looking into Paul Wonk's round face, thought she saw the wrinkled visage of a Golden Box Turtle with its turned up nose and little smile. The Wisdom of the Keeper had showed up to help. Paul left the platform.

The Tiger caught her eye and gave a wink.

Dr. Dierk returned to the podium and bowed to the delegation. "This concludes our presentation. Thank you for allowing our unscheduled demonstration."

The Tiger moved gently around Tug and came forward, eliciting a collective gasp from those in the front rows at the fearsome feline rising to His hind legs before them. He bowed His large banded head courteously to the assembly, paws together in sampeh, returned to all fours and beckoned with a paw to Tug. The child ran to Him, giggling. Dr. Dierk boosted him onto the Tiger's back.

"Remember, you are deciding the world this child will grow up in," the Tiger said to the assembly. Only a few looked fearful this time when He spoke; perhaps most of the assembly heard His words and not just a soft growl.

The Tiger padded solemnly up the center aisle, followed by Dr. Dierk and the students. Wildlings fell in behind.

The moderator moved cautiously up to the podium and spoke into the sound-projector.

"Wait," he said.

The visitors stopped.

"Honored Tiger, esteemed professor-teacher and students, you gave eloquent counter to the Wilds Development Protocol we will soon consider. Could your delegation of underrepresented publics offer a counter proposal?"

Paul Wonk had suggested this could happen. The TRI-WAC Governing Ordinances prohibited new proposals offered by unauthorized parties—unless invited by a high official of the Assembly.

Keren knew from Paul's TRI-WAC class briefing that Vice Moderator Dong Jun sat on the Committee of Order, the Host Region Organizing Council and the Protocol Prescreening Selection Board. He had the undisputed right to offer this invitation.

Wilds Simulation had affected at least one important heart and mind.

Dr. Dierk returned to the podium, smiling. "Your Eminence, in hopes of such an invitation, we have prepared a modest proposal."

chapter twenty-two
LAST WAR OF WORDS

W hen the Wild Simulation broadcast began, Counselor Dred ripped off his HEAD. He would not be brainwashed by this Nature propaganda. As the Dominion High Counselor for Babel II security and the top-ranking official in the Inter-Babel World Security Collective, he had to remain cool and collected. Still his monitors blazed with Wilds scenery and sounds. Frantic wrist waves did not mute the sound or blank off the viz. "Damn hacker kids!" he said. Must be the same miscreants who engineered Dierk's escape.

I thought we had blasted that Nature Head out of the sky. How did he escape? Where did he go? How did he mobilize those cursed Wildlings worldwide?

Dred's Special Security Forces had met the Save-Our-Wilds marchers at the Citadel and dispersed the humans. But the Wildlings settled in at the Citadel grounds. Eagles and hawks entertained themselves with periodic sorties against the building, flying right at the transparent walls and then veering away, showing off their skills and terrifying the Yessers within.

At Dred's own Central Security Complex, a convocation of eagles soared upwards together and then dove towards Dred's tower, veering at the last possible decisecond in a synced arc away into the air.

This air terrorism had to stop!

He flipped his wrist tab and barked, "Get me High Air Command!"

Hundreds of sleek fighter ships and black hovercraft readied for launch from Air Security Bases.

"Prepare to engage in Dogfight Maneuvers!" Dred told the Air Commander. The air above the complexes filled with fighting machines.

"Ready to engage, Sir," the commander said.

Dred sensed dissension from the dark Force. *Fool! Would you shoot birds out of the sky?* hissed the inner Voice.

Should we not rid the earth of these screaming air polluters? Do we not please You when we destroy the birds of the air?

Destruction is pleasing—when done well, the Voice said. *If you shoot the birds now you will invoke worldwide riots. The entire population is besotted by the Enemy's Wildlings.*

Their protection is finished, Master. In just a few hectoseconds, they will be delisted.

NO. Not delisted—permanently protected. Permanently. Have you ignored the TRI-WAC, Dred? Do you not know what has happened there? You let Dierk slip through your hands. Now he wins the delegates hearts with pretty pictures and Wilds fairy tales.

Cold sweat poured down his face. Win hearts? What had he missed?

Our Influencers in Babel I.1.1 say Vice Moderator Dong has requested a counter Proposal to the Wilds Development Protocol. Your escapee Dr. Dierk is presenting it now.

Dred tabbed back to the TRI-WAC cam, his hands shaking. On screen a grinning Dong Jun, before the podium, one hand on the shoulder of that cursed Dr. Dierk. Behind them loomed an oversized Tiger and enough exotic Wildlings to fill a few Zo-Parks.

"...a modest proposal." Audio caught Dierk's words.

Dred's head throbbed. If Dierk succeeded, Dred would implode from the fury of the Dark Forces.

We will not ONLY shoot a few birds, he told his Master. Our Enemy has given us unprecedented opportunity. S/HE has sent Wildlings right into our territory. We can bring about massive extirpation, before the TRI-WAC moves to protect them. Dierk's proposal will be worthless.

The dissent within him stilled. He felt a glimmer of dark approval. *Brilliant move, Counselor Dred.*

He glimpsed a cacophony of destructive visions: flaming missiles, burning corpses of Wildlings lining the streets, humans gaping at the show. The High Security weaponry could remove all traces of the Wildlings within a couple of hectoseconds.

Having postponed his own destruction, the High Counselor ordered up a Dominion Protocol planned for the unthinkable—a world war, an alien incursion, or an antiurban attack on the Babels.

"Dominion Human Security Command—Red Alert." His words coursed through HEADs and tabs of every urban security commander on the planet. "Mobilize all air and ground forces, auto-missile defense and robo-troops. In two kiloseconds, all deadly force will focus on the Wildling invaders. You will seek out and destroy all nonhuman life within the city perimeters. I repeat, in two kiloseconds, seek out and destroy!"

Throughout the world, military personnel sprang up from the gatherings around the monitors, fixated on the glowing red on wrist tabs. They let go joy and awe and refocused on their primary purpose: protection of urbanity. They filed onto Autos, headed for command posts.

In a thousand cities, automated war robots clicked "On," lit up, came to life and joined human counterparts in orderly rows of a worldwide war machine. In secret silos, panels slid open and gleaming missiles emerged, programmed to seek and destroy nonhuman and Wildling species. People would be exempted. Every other animal in the Babels would be annihilated.

Bill Benson turned to his wife in amazement. "Can you believe what Caleb's class did?" he enthused. "They've turned the whole world upside down. Dr. Dierk's about to offer a proposal to protect the Wilds."

Nora paled. "What is it, Nora?" her father asked.

"What about the Dominion?" she asked. "They aren't going to take this well."

"The Dominion has been stifled, for once," Bill Benson said. "The Wild Experience Sim overrode every transmission on earth." He motioned to the viz of Dr. Dierk addressing the TRI-WAC with a beaming Vice Moderator standing by.

"The Dominion still has force and weapons and..." Nora broke off.

RORRRRRRRRRRRR! KACHUNG! ZZZZZZZZZZZZZ-ZOOOOOOOMMMM!

"That's a fighter launch!" Nora screamed. "It's a Red Alert," she added. "I remember it from Military Science."

The ever-vigilant Newsflash shifted viz to gleaming black air ships converging on the winged Wildlings around City Center.

"Are they going to fire on the Wildlings?" Bill Benson asked.

"We have to stop this," Mrs. Benson said. She held out her hands. Nora laid aside skepticism and joined her parents in their counter-offensive.

"Keeper, see the forces of evil sent to destroy life from this planet," Mrs. Benson prayed. "We stand against them. Send out a greater life to swallow up Death."

Throughout the Babels, other families heard the roar of warplanes and joined in the plea. In a place where life began and returned, the call was heard.

Dr. Dierk summed up the provisions of the proposed Need-for-Nature Law to the attentive TRI-WAC delegates. "The Law will provide for expanding the Wild Preserve System and replacing Pocket Parks with Mini-Nature Preserves in every human settlement," he said. "An Access Portal will allow everyone to experience Wilds at any time. A Wilds visitation..."

HMMMMMMMMMMM interrupted his words. Robo-hovercraft, bristling with rockets and rapid-fire guns, filled the air around the Tower. Chamber doors flung open and a pod of war robots entered, blasters trained on the Wildlings.

"They are going to shoot the Wildlings," Arana gasped. Irving and Cynthia frantically punched their tabs, seeking the military frequency for a system override. "They've got an anti-intervention program, we can't hack it," Irving reported a long hectosecond later. "They fire in about... uh...half a kilosecond."

The Great Tiger strolled to the podium. This time everyone understood His voice. "World delegates to the Tri-Annual Convention, you represent all humanity and have authority over this planet. We will not override your authority.

"The military force of your Dominion will destroy Wildlings on earth. Wilds will vanish, urbanity will be reasserted, and the unlimited economic expansion will continue. Do you wish this?"

A great silence fell over the chamber. Delegates eyed the waiting war robots.

Babel I 1.1 Delegate Wang Hu and Deputy Dong Jun exchanged urgent whispers. Delegate Wang suddenly rushed to the side of the Great Tiger.

"Honored Tiger, we do not wish this! Our children deserve better! We are helpless against the forces we have released. Please help us!"

"HELP US. HELP US. HELP US," the delegates repeated, a growing roar of human voices filling the chamber. A voice began to sing, then others. Shouting turned to song, inspired by invisible Guides hovering among them. Space between the physical world and the worlds beyond filled with the sound of millions of voices, the soul-song of humans.

Caleb and Keren recognized the Song from the Desert Meadow, and the music of the Great Dance. Humans and Wildlings in the great assembly chamber joined morning stars and heavenly bodies in a song of the universe, ancient and endless. The Song grew with the voices of earth families singing against the powers of destruction.

The Song became a great Sound, an intense resonance, attuned against the forces of death.

War robots in the assembly hall shattered. Rockets and firing mechanisms on the hovercraft disintegrated, and fell in a shower of fragments.

The Song entered at a frequency tuned to destroy the alloy that composed modern armaments, rendering them harmless.

Throughout all Babels, the Song soared sweet, strong and vibrant— disintegrating weapons worldwide. Militia men and women gaped, stumbled or fainted as high-powered projectile rifles shattered in their hands; pilots fought to control bucking airships knocked around by the force of shattering missile casings.

"No weapon forged against you will stand," Dr. Dierk mused. "I will beat your swords into plowshares...I guess it's the same idea. Creative use of physics, Great Keeper," he said.

The Tiger smiled, showing sharp white gleaming teeth. "Delegates of the TRI-WAC, you have a proposal awaiting your decision. Distinguished Vice Moderator?"

Dong Jun wiped his brow and returned to the podium. "Do I hear a motion to pass the new Need-for-Nature Law?"

"So moved!" called Delegate Wang. "So seconded!" said the lead delegate from Babel II.

After a unanimous vote, Vice Moderator Dong offered a new order. "I hereby issue a weapon cleanup in every Babel. Here in Babel I 1.1, TRI-WAC delegates will lead the cleanup. Peacekeeper forces and Security Yessers are commanded to assist."

A small box tortoise left the Wildlings and slowly waddled up to Dong at the podium. The official bent low so the creature could whisper in his ear. "Ah yes, splendid suggestion, Honorable Tortoise," Dong said.

"In addition, future TRI-WACs will begin *not* with fireworks, promo viz and military parades. Instead, every Babel will host a Litter Pick-up and Park Walk for any citizens who wish to celebrate. In the conference city, delegates will lead the cleanup."

Vice Moderator Dong then recessed the TRI-WAC for ten kiloseconds so delegates and Wildlings could gather up the weapon fragments from the hall and the Tower grounds. Janitorial Yessers arrived with sweepers and blow-bags. Wildlings and dignitaries went to work.

Outside the Tower, adults and children labored in the warm spring sunshine, entertained by Wildling coworker antics. The chimps and gorillas excelled at corralling the metal pieces—although they couldn't resist tossing a few at the panthers and tigers, crouched low and using their paws to bat fragments into piles.

Tug rode the Great Tiger as He patrolled the cleanup operation. "Back to work, rowdies," the Tiger growled at the primates.

"It's better to throw metal than what we usually throw," quipped one monkey.

Lizzie, overhearing, said, "Ew." She had seen monkeys at Zo-Parks throwing poop at visitors.

"You are guests, and need to mind your manners," said the Tiger.

A great ape swung down from the trees and grabbed Tug from the Tiger's back, tucking him under his arm. "Tarzan, Tarzan!" shrieked the child as the ape swung back through the tropical foliage at the foot of the Super Trees.

"I think Tug has given up his military aspirations," Keren said, nudging Caleb to get his attention.

"Maybe he found something more interesting than shattered war robots and missiles," Caleb said. "He wanted adventure, and he got it."

"He should sleep well tonight," Keren said.

Taking a break from shuttling garbage, Keren took a peek at Newsflash updates. Soldiers and citizens worldwide had jumped on the cleanup orders with relief and joy. Pilots landed fighters and hovercraft, troops left their command posts, and families poured into the streets. Security Yessers rushed to collect blow-bags and sweepers. Wildlings joined the cleanup efforts.

Reporter Noreen Nose had dug up official reactions to the pro-Wild shift in opinions. She poked her tab towards Dr. Prudentia Freud, seated on a bench basking in warm spring sunlight. "Too much exposure to sunlight and air could be harmful to civilized human beings," Dr. Freud said. "But it is quite pleasant."

"Dr. Rich, what are the economic impacts of the Wild Protection Law?" Ms. Nose asked the other faculty member plopped on the bench alongside Freud.

"I'm concerned about distilling our economic energy with this new push for urban naturalism," said the famous economist as he unconsciously stroked the fur of a coatimundi. "But perhaps the reconstruction could become a new economic engine."

"In related developments, proactive deal-makers are already moving to capitalize on the new nature movement," said Newsflash anchor Archie Ash.

The cam swept back to Noreen Nose, now questioning developer-king Lester Noblitts as he swept up weapon fragments in Puddicombe Pocket Park.

"The World Developer League is developing a proposal to redevelop natural parks throughout the Babels," Noblitts said, "Parks can offer open air mini-Wilds opportunities with Demo Forests or Demo Deserts and natural ranges for selected Wildlings. We can replace the artificial Zo-Parks with truly Wild experiences right in the city."

Ms. Nose raised her eyebrows. "Mr. Noblitts, where will you get expertise to create Wild experiences in the Babels? Very few people know about the Wilds."

Noblitts grinned. "We have our own down-home expert in Babel II," he said. "Dr. Dierk, OA Biology teacher. We hope to cut a deal so Dierk can serve as consultant to the parks project. We want his expertise to design high-end mini-Wilds expeditions."

Lizzie turned from the monitors, her face registering mock horror. She put up her hands in a block motion towards Dr. Dierk, who was loading scraps into a bag held by a lars gibbon and apparently oblivious to the broadcast.

"Dr. Dierk, you're the new travel planner and park redeveloper," she said. "How will you find time to teach OA Biology?"

Dierk filled the bag, zipped it off and gave it to the gibbon for disposal. "I've already heard from our Deputy Administrator Mr. Snark," he said. "He wants a Demo Wild on the MERC grounds. We need to beef up the OA Biology staff, and he's already writing an ed grant for it. Biology is the new fad, and we'll be ready for it."

No doubt Yessers would be in the forefront of the New Nature Movement.

Members of the Dominion and their Security Counselors holed up in their secret command centers. The lords of the destructive world order argued and accused.

Behind them Dark Forces screamed, cursed and fought. Confused and angry, the Energizer fueled the rage, overwhelmed by failure. *Our finest deceptions are exposed! Our greatest weapons, ruined! And you indulge in brawling and temper tantrums! Our plans are set back decades and you will pay.*

Counselor Dred pulled away from his colleagues, and decked the Supreme Authority of the Babel II Dominion with a flick of his powerful wrist. "Fools," he said. "Don't you see we are playing right into the hands of our enemies? This is what the Keeper wants—to unleash our Force upon ourselves until we are consumed by it."

The feeling of brain cells exploding subsided. *You have just tasted your destiny, High Counselor Dred,* warned the Voice that haunted his every thought. *But you are correct. We do not need to destroy those who serve Us. It is time to regroup.*

The Keeper has turned the hearts of humanity. For a little while.

But we know the human heart. The Energizer chuckled. *The heart is fickle and it will turn. We will be ready.*

Counselor Dred felt relief, replaced by horror as the explosions in his head resumed, accompanied by visions: ugly wormlike creatures devouring his body, a white-hot fire burning through his veins, visages of destruction tearing at his skin with needle-like fingers. The screams around him told him that his companions also experienced the nightmare. The torture would leave no mark on the bodies of its victims, but they would carry inner scars that would never heal.

To the Energizer, the pleas of its tormented subjects made a sweet song, slowly calming its sense of humiliation and defeat in waves of pleasure. Over the eons, it had learned to soothe itself with human anguish and to feed itself on human pain. Only when the whole world joined this chorus of anguish would the Energizer be satisfied. Satiated by pain, it returned to its dream of deconstructing the Keeper's creation.

chapter twenty-three
NEW NATURE MOVEMENT

With the EU grounds clear of metal, the Tiger motioned to the assembled Wildlings. Small and large, the creatures bowed in unison to the delegates, Yessers and students. Then they ambled out through the broken walls. Keren wondered how they would get home.

"You know, child, that transport is not a problem for the Keeper," the Tiger said. He crouched down beside Keren and Tug dismounted, running to his big sister. Keren gave him a big hug and held him close.

The Tiger addressed Keren and Caleb. "You will see Us again," He said.

He bowed graciously to the assemblage of delegates and students, bounded over the TRI-WAC walls and disappeared.

Tug fell asleep before the Guides whisked them home, and didn't stir when Keren tucked him gently into his coverlets. She ran downstairs to her waiting parents. No need for a cover-up—their exploits had shown on Newswatch. She just wanted to fill in the details.

For the Andersons and other families, Sunday evening filled with questions, gasps, and excited chatter as the adventurers told their families about their Wild adventures.

By Monday, the TRI-WAC had passed a series of new laws amplifying the Need-for-Nature Law, including rights to visit Wilds, Pocket Park Re-Naturalization, and a change in mission for the Ranger Service.

Morning Newsflash showed scenes of Wildlings leaving the Babels, homebound for the Wilds. Drone cams caught furtive movements of animals slinking through the brush, cautious and shy. Future Wildling viewings would be a rare, delightful surprise.

Wilds fever had caught on. Ad channels carried a new slogan, "Nature is the new face of urbanity" with a shot of the Tiger strolling through the tropical forest arboretum with Tug riding on His back.

"A little child shall lead them," Dr. Dierk said as they watched the TRI-WAC proceedings—and the new ads—from the OA Biology classroom monitor.

Keren felt mortified at the notion of Tug as symbol for the new nature movement, but amused at the irony. "If the Tiger can tear Tug away from his war weapons, maybe he is a good symbol for our future," she said.

"Don't worry, Keren," Caleb gave her a playful punch. "I bet even Dr. Dierk played soldier as a little boy."

"Yup," said Dr. Dierk, saluting the class. "Until I got drafted for a more important battle. Just like you."

He pointed to the World Diagram showing encroaching Babels and shrinking Wilds. "Believe me kids," he said. "Our battle has just begun!"

The End

acknowledgments

To my mother, the late Helene Lewis "Mickey" Coffer, my lifelong inspiration, an intrepid reporter and persistent freelance fiction writer who sent countless proposals to her agent before she hit gold with published short stories and a romance book. She also taught me early to value a good editor: I still remember the first editorial I ran by Mom; it came back covered with red pen corrections! To my husband David, the king of storytellers, for natural history review and much of the whimsy of this book—my champion who always has believed in me. To my daughter and sisters, for artistic, creative and marketing inspiration in the formation of this book. To Ann Beltran, who walked with me on the early transition path from 9-to-5 careers to book authors. And to Tony, who loved my book in the early stages and eagerly asked for more chapters; I hope you love the whole book, too! To my professors at University of Arizona School of Journalism, long retired or even gone: Don Carson and your notorious "automatic E" assignments that taught me to get it right, and Jackie Sharkey for believing in my talent and always offering a friendly welcome at my "home" department. To Pat Sheehan and Vern Fridley, who allowed an "outsider" into the Forest Service and changed my career story. To my excellent editor, Michele Redmond, who has improved almost everything I have written over the past 10 years. To Mark Kashino, Hailey artist who helped me refine the artistic concept for this book. And finally to the staff at Morgan James Publishing: first and foremost Lara Helmling, acquisitions and copy editor, who "got" my book immediately and has championed my vision from the start; David Hancock for friendly personal support for every new author and book; and the rest of the creative team for your structure and encouragement in guiding my transition from generalist writer to fiction author.

about the author

Cindy C.'s childhood dream was to write books in a secluded mountain cabin. She got her start as editor of her high school newspaper and as cub reporter on her hometown newspaper in Oklahoma. The joy of writing to tell people's stories convinced Cindy to be a newspaper reporter and get paid to write. She got a journalism degree from University of Arizona (although her mother claimed she majored in hiking) and then worked for newspapers in Oregon and Utah. She spent her spare time outdoors with husband David, her best hiking buddy. To merge her twin passions for writing and the wilderness, Cindy pursued a master's degree in environmental politics and volunteered her way into a career with the USDA Forest Service. She then worked with David on international forestry projects in Cambodia and Lebanon. Today she resides in Hailey, Idaho, near Sun Valley Ski Resort and is manager of the newly founded Wilderness Need Association. Cindy's childhood dream of writing books from a secluded mountain cabin has evolved into life in a small mountain town where she writes about the wilderness. Return to the Wilds channels Cindy's experiences of nature and her passion for the environmentally ethical—and loving—treatment of the land. She is published and quoted as Cindy C. Chojnacky.

Morgan James
Speakers Group

↗ www.TheMorganJamesSpeakersGroup.com

We connect Morgan James published
authors with live and online events
and audiences who will benefit
from their expertise.